# *Praise for Redemption*

"I learned very early in life that the strangest things in life were often very real."

Lindsey Gray's Redemption is a riveting story that manages to entertain from beginning to end. Even as its different phases are revealed, it leaves us just as captivated by the lingering mystery at the end as we were right from the very first page. Ms. Gray takes us on an exciting ride into an alternate universe where the forces of good and evil are actively among us, and yet quietly at battle.

The mystery behind Lily Edwards' past and her current connection to the powerful, yet secretive Manchester Group quickly transforms into a web of relationships we are eager to explore. Exactly what is it "the Big Guy" has planned for her and those she loves? By the end, we are allowed to see with increasing clarity that not everything is as it seems.

Morality isn't just about who or what a person is, but rather the choices one makes from what is presented to us by fate and life; or is it the "Big Guy" upstairs? Nicely paced, the romance carries us through slightly darker moments where the life or death struggle leads to both love and sacrifice.

This story has all the mystery and intrigue of La Femme Nikita, mixed with the interconnected love and light angst of Charmed -- with a bit of 007 fun thrown in for good measure. All in all, Ms. Gray has produced a deliciously cinematic literary experience. What begins as a seemingly simple romance, full of aching longing, desire, and the promise of patience rewarded, quickly becomes a gripping adventure to rescue loved ones and save the world from the return of an evil thought to be previously leashed.

D.M. Undeberg ~ The Review Lounge

Lindsey Gray

# Redemption

The Writer's Coffee Shop
Publishing House

First published by The Writer's Coffee Shop, 2011

The Writer's Coffee Shop
(Australia)   PO Box 447 Cherrybrook NSW 2126
(USA)   PO Box 2116 Waxahachie TX 75168

Paperback ISBN- 978-1-61213-038-5
E-book ISBN- 978-1-61213-039-2

A CIP catalogue record for this book is available from the US Congress Library.

Cover image by: © Lindsey Gray
Cover design by: Lindsey Gray

www.thewriterscoffeeshop.com/lgray

# About the Author

Lindsey Gray was born with a fascination for the written word. By the time she was 12 years old, she had typed several short stories on her parents' Apple IIE computer. Like many young writers, her early aspirations were eclipsed by everyday life. The itch to write has always lingered and over the last few years her desire to create has grown to the point it can no longer be denied. She returned to her, now up-to-date, computer and the words flowed in to what has become her first published romance novel, Lies Inside. Shortly after, she decided to take her hand at another genre and delved into the supernatural with the first in her series of novels, Redemption.

# Dedication

To my family and friends. I pay homage to you with my words for your tremendous inspiration and encouragement.

*Prologue*

A small, carbon steel blade in the hands of a sadistically cruel animal, was all that stood between her and the only family she had ever known. He had his victim's hands and ankles tied down to the steel chair in the center of the blackened room.

Lily kept her distance, for fear that any movement she made would make his hand slip, causing the blade to torment his victim further. She could see he was enjoying the emotions seeping into the room; hate and fear exuded from her every fiber. His exhilaration traveled swiftly through him as he reveled in looming over his victim. The tip of his knife caressed the thin sheet of skin that covered her jugular vein, as his tongue slipped across to moisten his more than perfect lips.

The blade caught a tear from his victim's cheek before it had a chance to fall; its taste so sweet as he wiped the blade across his tongue and stimulated each taste bud.

"Time is running out. Blood will be spilt whatever you decide, you need only to choose whose it will be."

Lily had a choice to make. She knew she had only moments before he would carry out every threat he had promised to. His one demand was the only thing holding her back.

She took one last long look over him. His eyes, still the same deep blue piercing through her from within the shadows. His smile, still just as perfectly charming. When she looked deeper, she saw something in him more clearly than she ever had before; his soul. Black and corrupted by words she was sure he himself almost certainly didn't comprehend.

Her eyes narrowed, her jaw clenched. "They will kill me if I do this." Her words were resolute, but her voice trembling at the incredulous truth of it all.

"Then you have a decision to make. Whose existence is more important?" He brought his cheek next to his victim's, sealing a tear upon it with a kiss. "Hers or your own…?"

Before he could let the last breath pass through his lips, she replied. "Hers."

# Chapter One

## Transition

Her hardened flesh was colder than usual. Her body had become accustomed to the Icelandic winters, but even she thought this arctic breeze was ridiculous.

"A hundred years. You'd think I'd be used to the cold by now," Lily thought to herself, as she precariously watched her steps across the ice.

She had been stalking a mountain goat for twenty minutes. She took her time as she headed for solid ground. As soon as she felt the earth replace the ice beneath her feet, she was off running like gossamer; her chestnut tendrils flying in every direction as she gained speed. She pounced on the goat, not giving it any chance to fight back before she shredded the jugular vein. She drank in every drop of sweet deliciousness she could before the heart could no longer pump it. The poor goat never stood a chance.

Lily's thirst had become all consuming as of late. Some close calls with the wrong type of prey precipitated her relocation to Iceland. It was easy for her to get lost in a country of only three hundred thousand. Twenty hours of darkness on most winter days gave her the perfect opportunity to blend in and hunt without discovery – the ideal setting for a vampire to survive.

Lily made the short five mile trek back to her home. A modest, but comfortable house that was perfect for her existence. She tried to keep it simple. She had only traveled with a few things, leaving the rest in storage in the States. This move had become increasingly more permanent than she had hoped, and she was longing for a few comforts that were lying dormant in a Massachusetts storage unit.

She had enjoyed her visits to the Icelandic north over the years, but it was always more of a holistic retreat than a final resting place. After the year she had been through she had more than enough retreating to do to remain the vampire she needed to be.

Lily stood in her entryway, dripping with red tinted snow as she discarded her hunting gear. Firstly, her boots, one of her most prized possessions, with leather laces that stood up to any type of weather. Then her down jacket, which had become more of a comfort than a necessity. She paused briefly when her eyes noticed a few specks of frozen crimson blood soaked into the fabric. *"No worries,"* she thought. She had more than enough years of experience removing blood stains from any type of material. After she tossed it aside, she made her way to the bathroom.

This is where she slipped into her ritual of removing the rest of her clothes. The stiff thermal shirt, followed by ice crusted jeans and slightly damp socks, which protected her flawless pedicure. Her black lace bra and panty set were the last items to hit the floor before she entered the steaming hot shower.

Even though her body never radiated any type of heat, she was extremely sensitive to it. The warm water washed over her with a soothing effect as the steam brought the hair on her body to attention. It was an extremely cathartic experience. One she repeated twice daily.

Reluctantly, she turned off the water. A fluffy, pink bathrobe beckoned her from the hook on the back of the bathroom door. She toweled off before slipping the cotton candy body suit over her newly warmed skin.

Her couch was particularly inviting after the vigorous hunt of the evening. She stretched out across the leathery goodness, only to find her journal tucked between the cushions. She pulled the onyx colored book from the grip of the couch, her fingers trailing across the golden numbers scrolled across it.

"What a hideous year."

She would have never made homage to that year except for the fact she had made one for every other year of her existence. Memories etched in eternity. Some she would never forget, others she would be glad to do so.

The past year was the kind of year she dreaded, the transition year. The better parts of the previous five years were spent around Portland, Oregon. She had passed for twenty-five when she arrived and had left when it became increasingly difficult to pass as a convincing thirty year old.

Being eternally twenty-five had its advantages. She could pass for as young as eighteen or as old as thirty. For the most part, she was able to control her thirst around humans.  This enabled her to stay in one place for an extended period of time.  It became time to leave Portland and start somewhere new.

She flipped open the cover of the journal to find the first entry.  She rang in the New Year in Las Vegas – another city that never slept and she had slipped into the adrenaline based atmosphere with ease.  Even though iguanas were not very sustaining, she had felt comfortable in the desert, for a while.

It was in her nature to control her urges, but the time came for her to feel good to be bad.  The city brought out her seductive side, which was never a good thing for a vampire.  Even though she had no need for a career, she was in Sin City and she had the body for it.

She laughed as she came across a picture of her Vegas alter ego, Cinnamon.  The name screamed showgirl, at least to her.  She had walked into the hottest club on the strip for an audition – a formality at the very least.  Her long flowing chestnut curls danced across her milky white skin and once the owner caught a glimpse of her cinnamon stare, he would have given her anything she wanted.

ε ϒ ʓ

"So, what do you say?"  Lily asked, flashing her smile that would melt butter.

"I think I have something for you."  He winked back at her while he wiped his hand through his greasy goatee.

"A few conditions though."

"You think you can give me conditions?  Look, sweetheart. I'm the boss, you're the stripper."

"Dancer," she corrected him.

"Whatever, but my customers pay for a full show.  I'll be expecting at the very least what I've seen today.  They'll expect much more."

"Fine, just listen for a minute, please," she said, pulling the chair next to him, and swiveling it around.  She came down on the chair backwards, inching it close to him.  Her sweet breath filled the inches between them as she spoke again.  "I will most definitely be one of the best you've ever seen.  I will have your customers stuffing so much money into this club, you'll think you're the King of Siam.  But…no private dances.  Only with another girl and a bouncer present.  No groping and absolutely, no kissing."

He licked his already moist lips.  "That sounds reasonable, only if you start tonight."

"Deal."

ଝ ᐻ ଧ

She was in for a real change. Her nights were filled with cognac soaked bills passed to her G-string from lawyers, doctors, and very dirty politicians. Her couples dances with the other girls actually became very popular. She hadn't really realized how much it turned a man on to just sit back and watch.

Lily had no problem controlling her thirst when it came to the girls. The men all had collectively a different scent. Some sweet, others musky. One smelled exactly like the oil from a nineteen fifty-seven Bel Air. He reminded her why she loved cars so much over their hour long conversation. It retrieved all her memories of Martin, her sire.

By late May, she thought it might not be so bad after all. She could spend a couple of years living out her wildest fantasies. She didn't need much sleep and she fed when she could. It was glorious exercise, even though she had no need for it. As she always kept her body sharp, and her mind even sharper.

ଝ ᐻ ଧ

"Got a request for you, Miss C. You and Samantha in the blue room, now." The greasy manager shouted into their dressing room as if the entire world needed to hear.

"I'm on the main stage in five minutes. Can't it wait?" Lily combed her hair back into a seductive sweep while rolling her eyes.

"No it can't. If you want to keep yourself employed, you'll get your ass in there now."

"Alright!" Samantha screamed as she pulled Lily from her chair. "Come on, C. We'll do the Double Dutch. It won't take too long."

"As soon as the butterscotch comes out, they're already halfway there." Lily's lips parted to expose her glossy white teeth. They both snickered as they made their way to the blue room.

He sat alone in the high-backed leather chair provided for him. His smoldering blue eyes enveloped all that was Lily. His lips created a coy smile while showing off his alabaster teeth. Not the usual customer, draped in a tailored black suit with electric blue button down shirt. Looking barely old enough to even be there, no more than twenty-two, with dark hair cropped short behind his ears. There wasn't even a hint of a glance at Samantha. This left Lily a bit unsettled, but intrigued as well.

"We can get started as soon as Sonny takes his seat." Lily spread out the black tarp across the hard marble floor as Samantha retrieved the supplies from behind the bar. His eyebrow rose slightly as his stare stayed on Lily. She glided her fingertips lightly across her left breast to gauge what kind of man she was dealing with. He continued to sit in silence, but she knew she was having an effect on him. He may have been sitting perfectly still, but his heart was beating wildly in his chest.

Sonny entered and took his seat, nodding to the girls. They began their routine with some light nuzzling at first. Samantha's body heat began to warm Lily's icy flesh and they pressed their bodies together like fire and ice. A seductive chill ran down their intertwined bodies. He sat motionless, only a bead of sweat running from his forehead.

"Time to take care of business," Samantha chimed, as she reached for the butterscotch. Surprisingly, the mystery man shifted his position, and she wondered if she was finally getting to him.

As Samantha stepped on the tarp, she slipped, falling back to the floor. Lily sprung to her side a little too fast, as Sonny and the mystery man hurried to her as well.

"Can you move?" Lily asked, as she caressed Samantha's face.

"I'm fine. I think I pulled something, though."

"I'll take her back to the dressing room and send in Lexus." Sonny stated, as he lifted Samantha to her feet. "Can I trust you'll keep your hands to yourself?" The mystery man nodded in affirmation as Sonny carried Samantha out through the black curtain.

Lily folded up the black tarp and stowed it back behind the bar.

"I hope you don't mind if we change things up a bit. Lexus and I usually do something a little less...sticky." He just smiled with the piercing gaze emanating from his eyes. He pulled off his jacket and hung it on the back of his chair.

She pulled Sonny's chair to sit in front of her customer. She sat, legs crossed, arms wrapped around her chest trying to hold in what was left of Samantha's heat.

"Not a man of many words, are you?"

"No." His voice resonated in her ears, his breath trailed till it met her cheek.

"This opportunity doesn't come cheap. I would hate for you not to get your money's worth."

"I already have."

"So, spreading out a tarp in my G-string was enough?"

"Walking in from behind that curtain was almost enough."

Lily's mind began to race. His voice was so soothing, an effect rarely brought upon her by any human.

*What kind of game is he playing?*

"I've been watching you, here at the club. I've noticed something." He reached his hand to stroke her cheek but she quickly pulled back. "I'm not going to bite."

"We have a strict 'hands off' policy."

"Just one touch?"

She inched her face closer as his chair slid forward across the marble floor. His hands made their way to either side of her face, his gaze was mesmerizing. She had no idea how long they stayed like that before he made the distance between them mere centimeters, his sweet breath playing tricks with her mind. She felt herself slip as his warm lips pressed against hers. She knew it was against the rules, *her rules*, but she couldn't make herself stop. His warmth entered through her mouth and traveled to her icy core.

*"What human could possibly have this kind of power over me?"* The thought reverberated through her mind as his lips finally retreated from hers.

"I know what you are." He placed a few more kisses on her now warmed lips before she realized what he had said.

He pulled back, gently caressing her chin with his fingertip. This pulled her out of the kiss induced, drugged state. "What am I?"

"Dead," he simply replied.

She raised her brows at him. "That seems like a very rude thing to say."

He pulled her hair back and swept it to one side and lightly traced his fingertip across the small scar on the back of Lily's neck. "I know what you have inside. Amazing how something so small can fool so many. Genius, really. A small electrical pulse and everyone believes you are what you pretend to be." He tried to place another kiss on her neck, but she pulled away.

"Maybe I shouldn't have stayed." She attempted to lift herself from the chair when he grasped her wrist.

"I want to help you. I'd be a loyal companion."

"I think you've had a little too much to drink."

"Here, I'll make it easy for you." He took a pocket knife from his pocket, rolled up his sleeve and instantly slashed the top of his forearm.

Lily jumped back out of her seat. "You shouldn't have done that. You have no idea what you're getting yourself into."

He rose from his seat and walked toward her, offering the arm that dripped with crimson delight. "I want you to. I think if you take a taste, you'll realize I'm right."

She continued to back away. Her eyes closed tightly, trying desperately to block out the smell her body yearned for. "You have no idea how long it's been."

"It's right here. Just take it."

His arm was only a millimeter from her lips. They parted as her tongue escaped her mouth and caught a drop of his offering. His young blood rejuvenated her body more than any iguana ever did. Her tongue made its way back and forth across the fresh wound until the blood had almost stopped flowing; almost. She knew she could get away with drinking more and was about to give in, to sink her teeth into the inviting flesh...

"I think that's close enough." They were both startled by Sonny's entrance. Lily snapped back into the realization of the situation and wiped her mouth, covering his arm with his sleeve.

"Lexus will be in soon."

"I can't." Lily turned to dart out of the room.

"Lily please, don't go." She turned; stunned that he knew her real name. He grabbed her wrist. She looked down at his grip, at the blood seeping through his shirt. She turned her arm and caught a glimpse of the inside of his wrist. A small, black circle of flames inked on his skin. The mark of a servant long since forgotten. It didn't matter though, she had to escape.

"Please." One last pleading look from her mysterious willing slave. She couldn't stand his adoring eyes warming every inch of her body.

The curtain flew as she almost invisibly made her way to the dressing room. She grabbed her things, jumped into a pair of jeans and a t-shirt, and sprinted out the door, her McLaren SLR ready and waiting. She thought how thankful she was that she had a full tank of gas, with a few spare canisters in the back. She couldn't stop, not now.

His blue eyes burned in her rear view mirror as she spun out of the parking lot.

She drove through the night and all the next day and made her way as far East as she could without stopping. Only three stops for gas before she made it to New England.

It was only a few weeks until she settled in Boston. She found herself working for the Boston office of The Manchester Group, but it wasn't what occupied most of her time.

ʕ ℀ ʓ

She flipped the journal to the page where the delicate paper napkin was attached. It had been almost two days since her last thought of him, but there was his phone number soaked in black ink on the napkin.

ʕ ℀ ʓ

Marty O'Shea's was the place to be on Wednesday nights, at least for her. She was addicted to amateur nights. Wednesday nights, Marty O'Shea's held one. That first Wednesday in July, she was trying her hardest to be nonchalant, but she was really aching for an audience. When you have nothing but time on your hands, music was a pretty good distraction.

She added her name to the roster of mostly testosterone filled, ivy league boys and sat patiently awaiting her turn while sipping her red wine.

"Everyone put your hands together for a first time performer and our only brave lady on the roster tonight. Give it up for Lily." The bartender patted her on the shoulder as she took her place on stage with her guitar.

As the music begun, the audience hollered at her choice. As soon as the lyrics began, three wannabe Irishmen started singing. She felt herself moving to the music, mouthing the words as the Irishmen belted them out. Her black t-shirt clung to her torso, fueling the hormone charged room. She found herself inviting the Irishmen up on stage to finish her set. When she was announced that nights winner, her three new best friends hoisted her in the air.

Her fingers drifted across the picture of the three of them with her on their shoulders. She flipped to the next page, to a picture of her with Ian.

She usually shied away from emotional and physical relationships with humans, as she never wanted a repeat of her Vegas mystery man. But there was no escaping Ian's cerulean blue eyes. Not that she hadn't been attracted to men before; every time was different. Most men couldn't escape her beauty, a curse more than a blessing. Ian wanted more.

Ian worked as a concert pianist since he had finished his Master's of Music in Piano Performance from The Boston Conservatory. Every time his fingers hit the keys, he struck something that had lain dormant inside her for so many years, and she couldn't help but feel herself falling.

She explained her aversion to sunlight and her pale complexion fairly easily – a mild form of Solar Urticaria, an allergy to direct sunlight. That got her out of the weekend baseball games and afternoon barbeques. It wasn't that she couldn't handle direct sunlight. She wouldn't burst in to flames and turn into ash or any such nonsense; it was just uncomfortable at times and was better to avoid it as much as possible.

So, after three months of meeting under the cover of darkness, he begged for a weekend away. Luckily, the weekend expected drizzle for all forty-eight hours. Giving into the mood of the weather, she suggested a weekend in Salem.

October in Salem was promising. A trip to haunted houses and a physic fair before settling in at a bed and breakfast. It got him into an expectantly spooky mood. She tread lightly as she approached the subject of the paranormal.

"What do you think…about all this stuff?"

"Oh, I love it. Scary movies, the houses, the whole bit. I love October."

"I mean, do you believe in it? Witches, magic and stuff?" She was failing miserably to get her point across.

"I don't know. But being here, it's hard not to." She could tell that Ian had other notions on his mind as he playfully grabbed her hand and threw her down on the bed.

He straddled her while ripping his shirt off and exposing the abs of possibly a Greek god. She strummed her fingertips across his ripped midsection, before grabbing him and flipping him over so she was on top. She reached for the camera that lay on the bedside table.

ଓ ᛉ ଧ

The picture was right before her. It caught his bare chiseled chest, inviting eyes and his dimpled, stubble covered cheeks. The words he had uttered next filled her with awe and relenting torture at the same time.

"Marry me?"

There was no response that could have done him any justice at that point. If she had a heart, it would have surely broken at that moment. She just dropped the camera and fell on top of him. She met his lips as his arms surrounded her, taking in as much of him as she could; now knowing she would have to leave him. She kept what raw emotions she hadn't already exposed in check, but she had to have him.

Each time they were together, she knew there was a danger. She couldn't help but crave his warmth inside of her. With each thrust, each moan, she wanted to keep them in the moment forever. She knew the instant her fingernail drew blood from his back as it was almost too much to bear. His climax came close to her breaking point.

She excused herself to find something to clean up his back. Rushing into the bathroom, she grabbed the rubbing alcohol, and doused her hand with it; removing every trace of blood before it was too late. She scrubbed his back of every drop before placing a large dressing over the scratch.

He took her exuberance as a positive answer to his question, even though she never said yes.

When they got back to Boston, Ian left her to call his buddies and family to break the happy news. Lily packed. She packed all of her accumulated cold weather gear. She had just sent for her portable storage unit from Portland and the boxes still lined her hallway. Luckily, her firm had a place to store what she needed to, including the McLaren. It was all in place.

Her townhouse was cleared out, her possessions tucked away where he couldn't find them. She laid a letter across the piano keys, knowing he would find it there. That was the day she left to return to her home in Iceland.

*How could I have let it go that far?* That picture was the last in the book. Now, when the year was hours from its end, she could lay the book to rest. She tucked it safely within the books on the mantle, between her well read novels.

The phone didn't even startle her when it finally rang. She knew Renee would call.

"Hello, Renee."

Renee spoke so fast that it was even hard for Lily to understand. Renee would be her family, if she had true family, the only other woman around twenty-five in the area. The end of the line came with screams of "You have to" and "It'll be the greatest night of your life." Lily couldn't protest any longer and agreed to meet at the bar where everyone, unfortunately, knew her name. Another new year.

She put on what she hoped would be her most unattractive ensemble. Comfy jeans, her boots, of course, her blue thermal, and a faded navy flannel shirt. No makeup or hair products, just a simple rubber band holding her hair together at the nape of her neck. She would appear as just one of the guys, she hoped.

## Chapter Two

## Hopeless

It had been two months, one week, four days, four hours, and thirteen minutes since he last saw her.

Ian sat on the piano bench in the den of the townhouse where he couldn't escape her. He had spent the better part of the last two months there, wondering what went wrong.

He took a swig from the bottle of red wine that sat beside him, one of the twenty she had left in the wine cellar. He pulled her letter from his pocket, turning it over and over in his hands before opening it for at least the thousandth time. The folds were barely keeping the cream colored paper together. He argued with himself whether or not to read it again. There couldn't be any more meaning in the words than what he had already acquired. His heart won out over his mind, as he began to read it once again.

> My Dearest Ian,
>
> There are no words to explain what I'm doing now. As you can see, the townhouse is practically empty. All that is left, I left for you. I know the piano isn't much, but I couldn't think of a better life for it than to have you stroking its keys everyday. It's yours if you want it.
>
> I didn't leave because you asked me to marry you and I didn't leave because I was scared of how much you loved me. I

*left because I am so scared of loving you. That love might actually hurt you more than you will ever know. For reasons that are beyond control, even our love can't protect us. I should say don't look for me, but I know you'll try. There is no one you know to ask, so I don't think you'll get very far. Just know that I am safe and now that I'm gone, you are too.*

*I know how much you love this place. I had already paid Manny through to May, so you are welcome to stay. His numbers are on the fridge. Call him if you decide to stay.*

*If someone would have told me a year ago that I would be this much in love, I would have laughed in their face. Then there you were and how could I resist you? It seems like forever since I really loved someone the way I love you. I just know if anything happened to you because of what I am, I could never forgive myself.*

*I will never forget you or a second of the time we spent together.*

*All my love,*
*Lily*

Even though he had every word memorized, he needed the letter in his hands. To keep the last piece he had of her, fragile and falling apart like he was.

He had called Manny the day after she left. He wasn't sure that he could ever leave.

After searching every inch of the townhouse and badgering every person he thought could have known her, he was still left empty. He was beginning to think she was right; he was never going to find her.

Every time his phone rang, his heart sped up. This time, it was just his mother.

"Hey, Mom."

"Honey, are we ever going to see you again?"

"Yes, mother."

"Are you practicing? Will you be ready for the concert?"

"Yes of course I'm practicing; I've been ready for this for years. You know that, Mom," he replied, rolling his eyes while taking a swig of wine.

"Are you going out tonight? It is New Year's Eve."

"I wasn't planning on it."

"Then come to the house. You know your father would love to see you. It's just not the same here without you knocking around in the guest house.

At least then, we saw you once a week. It's been over three weeks, honey. You didn't even make an appearance at Christmas."

He could tell she was worried, but really didn't feel like placating her at the moment.

"Mother, I'm in no shape right now to come to one of your parties."

"Oh, it's only about a hundred and fifty people. You'd know almost everyone."

"How many of them are single women in their twenties?" He took a swig, then swallowed hard.

"Well…"

"Forget it, mother. I can't. I just can't," he replied, effectively cutting her off.

"Staying in that townhouse isn't healthy, you know."

"I know, but it's the only place I feel close to her."

"What are you waiting for? She told you she wasn't coming back."

"No, she said I wouldn't find her, not that she wouldn't be back."

"I'll save the rest of this argument for another time. Just promise you'll come over before your next concert. I miss your playing in the music room."

"Yes, I'll be there. Enjoy your party."

"Happy New Year, darling."

"Happy New Year." Ian hung up the phone and grabbed the now empty wine bottle.

Making his way to the kitchen, he threw the bottle in the trash, and went to the wine fridge to retrieve another one.

A knock on the front door startled him and his feet dragged across the hardwood floor as he made his way to the door.

"Hey, Ian. Got a package for you."

"Hey, Charlie," he greeted Charlie, his mailman, while taking the package from him.

"Still no word on your Lily?"

"No, nothing yet."

"I have something that might help." Charlie dug through his bag until he found the envelope he was looking for. "I know I shouldn't be doing this, but it might help. I found it stuck in the back of my truck."

Ian took the envelope that was undeniably a cell phone bill. "Oh, Charlie, you've just given me the best Christmas present ever." Ian stated, as he reached out and hugged Charlie.

"I just hope it helps. Wish I could do more."

Ian pulled back and shook Charlie's hand vigorously. "I'm sure this will be more than I could have ever hoped for. Thanks."

"Happy New Year."

"I certainly hope so. You too."

Ian shut the door and ran back to the kitchen as fast as his feet could carry him. He threw the package filled with sheet music on the counter then ripped open the envelope. He slowly read through every number. His house, his cell. Her work, her secretary... Finally, there was one number he didn't recognize – area code five zero three.

Not thinking what to say, he dialed the number. His heart raced and his pulse took flight as the other end continued to ring. Then a click – voicemail.

"You've reach Rebecca Swift. I'm unable to get to my phone right now. If you don't leave me a message, I can't call you back. It's your decision."

He anxiously awaited the beep. "Hey, Rebecca, my name is Ian Holt. I'm a friend of Lily Edwards? She gave me your number to call in case I needed to get a hold of her. It's kind of an emergency, so if you could call me back at 617-555-2432 as soon as possible. That's 617-555-2432. Anytime, day or night. Thanks." He hung up the phone. Then it began, the long wait.

He decided to start the easy way. Google. He set up his laptop on the kitchen table and began to search. First, a reverse number look up. Nothing, except he found it was a Portland number. This prompted him to do a name search through The Portland Tribune home page.

He actually got three hits off the name Rebecca Swift. The first, an engagement announcement for a couple in their fifties. He discounted that one because the voice he had heard was much too young. The second Rebecca Swift, had placed as the runner up in the Miss Teen Portland pageant the previous year. Too young.

The third was an article about an FBI agent named Rebecca Swift. She was the lead on a federal murder case that had taken place at the Portland facility of The Manchester Group. *Bingo!* That was the same company that Lily had worked for in Boston.

He logged onto The Manchester Group homepage. He had never questioned Lily about her job, as she never thought it was that exciting. He had no idea the group had seven offices in the States and several scattered throughout the globe. This just brought on a whole new plethora of questions, ones he didn't know if he wanted the answers to.

He didn't know Rebecca; therefore, she must be able to help him. Lily had said, after all, that he didn't know anyone who would know where she was. Ian decided to make a list of all the things he did know about Lily. Which ones were true though?

She had told him that she was an only child. That she had lost her parents while she was still in college. She was left a substantial inheritance, but liked having a career. He never really understood what an investment banker did, but she seemed to enjoy it, so he never questioned it. She loved working for The Manchester Group because she was able to travel, one of her favorite obsessions. She had friends located all over the world. Her flexible schedule and large amount of funds at her disposal gave her the opportunity to travel often. Yet, since meeting Ian, she had never planned another trip.

As far as past romances, he only knew of one. She only ever talked about one; Ryan. She said they had met while she was visiting an old family friend in London. Ian assumed that that meant he was British. They had a short courtship, as she called it. They became engaged, but soon after, her parents died and she had to return to the States. After trying a long distance relationship for a while, she was settling the estate and trying to finish school, it just didn't work out. By the time she was done with school, it was too late for them. Very vague. He knew that wasn't the whole story, but didn't want to push it for fear of reopening old wounds.

Most of their time was spent in each others arms. Dancing in the moonlit garden behind the townhouse. Making love that was intensified by the soundtrack of her favorite composer, Vivaldi. Talking about adventures to Italy, France, Spain, Egypt, and of course there was London. She would sit, content, to just listen to him play for hours.

Then to the things he didn't know. He had never asked where she was born or what her parents' names were. Where she grew up or what schools she had attended. They just didn't seem that important at the time. He knew none of her childhood friends, but perhaps Rebecca was one of them.

He could hardly grasp the phone between his fingers as it rang. When he finally composed himself, he checked the caller ID. Rebecca.

"This is Ian," he answered before holding his breath.

"Ian? It's Rebecca Swift." A soft woman's voice beckoned him from the other end. He noticed how soothing it was and seemed to relax as he began.

"Thank you for getting back to me so quickly."

"Not a problem. I knew if it was about Lily, it must be important."

This intrigued him. Lily must be very important to Rebecca. "I needed to get a hold of Lily. She'd given me your number..."

"No she didn't. Lily would never give out my number," she replied, cutting him off.

He was completely busted. She must have talked to Lily about him and now he had no idea where to go next.

"She did say that if you found my number, you would call. Is that what happened?"

"You got me. I'm worried that's all."

"I know, she has been giving me fits lately too. I can assure you though; she's fine, wherever she is."

"So, you don't know?" He felt the last of his hope fall into the abyss.

"I don't know where she is, but I did talk to her today. That's why I thought it was so strange that you called today of all days."

"New Year's Eve?" He was confused as to why this day would be so special.

"You really don't know, do you?" Rebecca let a soft laugh escape her lips before adding, "It's her birthday."

Another thing he had never thought to ask, her birthday. "I had no idea."

"This must be a sign. I have the feeling that she's not doing well. I was about to come to Boston to see if I could pick up her trail."

"I'd love to help. I need to find her." He waited for her response which seemed like hours rather than seconds.

"I have some vacation time coming up. I can be there by tomorrow afternoon."

"You have no idea how grateful I am to you. I've been sitting about for two months with no hope until today."

"I don't know if it would make it worse to bring you along."

"Is she in some sort of danger? Do you know her because you're FBI?"

"You've been doing your homework. She's the reason I joined the FBI. It took a while for Lily to warm up to me, but once I got to know her, she became a wonderful friend."

"I didn't know she had friends." He stumbled over the words, not wanting to offend the only person in the world who could help him.

"She has me. If I weren't so pushy, she wouldn't even have that. She won't admit it, but she misses having someone to look out for her."

"She told me her parents had passed away. Is that true?"

"Yes, she lost her parents. I'm sure whatever she has told you about herself is mostly true. She likes to leave out little details though, mostly names and dates."

"I hadn't really noticed. There is so much I just never asked."

"Men are very distracted by Lily. I'm not surprised she was able to keep you in the dark."

"What's going on with her? One moment we were engaged, the next she was gone."

"You have to understand something about Lily, she doesn't commit. She thinks it's safer that way."

"Safer? What does she need to keep me safe from?"

"There are people who would love nothing more than to get their hands on Lily. I think they'd use anyone close to her as bait. That's why I'm not so sure you should come along. I don't know what she'd do if something happened to you."

"Is that how she lost her parents? Because of some mysterious threat?"

"She lost a man whom she thought of as a father. She promised herself she would never let what happened to Martin happen again."

Lily had never mentioned Martin to Ian. It was yet another thing he had no idea about. With all the things he had known and loved about her, he hoped all these new revelations would make him love her even more.

"I might not know what I'm getting myself into and I'm sure there is much more that you're not telling me...I'm in though, all the way. Tell me what to do."

"From what I got out of her today, I'd say pack for cold weather."

"Alaska, maybe?"

"Not exactly. I'll explain more when I get there. I'll call you when I land."

"You have no idea what this means to me."

"She means the world to me too. Just don't let me regret taking you along."

"I won't. Thanks, Rebecca."

"My friends just call me Becca."

"Becca, then. Tomorrow?"

"Tomorrow. Happy New Year."

"Yeah, you too."

ଧ ᛘ ଷ

Lily pulled her Jeep up to the front of the bar and stepped out cautiously. She felt that someone or something had followed her since she'd left the house. It had been a while since she'd had any trouble with any otherworldly characters, but she had a feeling her luck was about to run out.

She made her way to the door of the bar, and as it creaked open, the light flickered on.

"Surprise!" A crowd of bar dwellers yelled at the top of their drunken lungs.

Lily made her way through the crowd, trying to act surprised until she found Renee.

"You surprised?" Renee hugged Lily while jumping up and down in excitement.

"I could wake up tomorrow morning with my head glued to the carpet and I wouldn't be more surprised than I am right now."

Renee let go of her. "You're making jokes."

"You know me."

"Good. Present time. I have something to add to your movie collection." Renee grabbed a package wrapped in white Christmas paper from behind the bar. "I hope you don't have it already."

Lily ripped off the paper to reveal *The Jason Bourne Collection.* "You know me too well. I hadn't bought this yet."

"Yep, it's all three movies plus a bunch of extra stuff. Plus, I know how you have a thing for Matt Damon. I thought this would be better than the *Ocean's* collection, because you get to see more of Matt kicking ass."

"Thanks, it's perfect." She hugged Renee in thanks and caught the scent of seventy year old malt whiskey.

"You didn't..."

Renee grabbed the bottle from beneath the bar. "I don't know why you like this stuff, but Dad got a hold of it and knew you'd love it."

Erik made his way over to the two of them through the drunken crowd. His stocky build and salt and pepper hair were always a comfort to Lily. Erik swooped her up into a bear hug. "Happy birthday, sweetness. We're glad you didn't take off before we could give you a proper party this year."

In many years past, she had always ducked out by the thirty-first, knowing her cold weather family would want to make a spectacle of her birth. Little did they know how old she really was.

"How old are we actually this year?" Erik inquired, while going around the bar to pour her present.

"How old do I look?"

"You don't look a day over twenty-five, but I know you must be older."

"Nope, eternally twenty-five. I won't have it any other way." Lily grinned as she saw the whiskey slowly poured into the glass. *One finger, two fingers, three fingers, four...*

One of Lily's only human pleasures that she would partake of on a regular basis was the fine gift of alcohol. It was the only thing besides blood that had any flavor for her, as her taste buds had a very limited range. For some reason, single malt whiskey was one of her favorites.

She reached for the glass, pressed it to her lips and let the scent engulf her senses. The aroma tantalized every muscle, played with every cell and danced with every fiber. She let a mouthful slip down her throat, enveloping her mind and body.

"Mmmmmmmm... A very good birthday. Thanks, Erik."

"You're welcome, sweetness. Now, as they say, let's get this party started."

The bar's lights went down and a tremendous light show began.  Colors sparkling off the crystal ball that had replaced the antler chandelier.  Music boomed from a large speaker in the corner as Erik was now playing DJ. Lily hugged Renee while pulling her to the dance floor; because if Lily was dancing, everyone else would have to join in.

## Chapter Three

## Discovery

After he searched the townhouse for over an hour in vain, Ian realized that almost everything he needed for an arctic trek was sitting in his parent's guest house. He begrudgingly accepted the fact that in order to retrieve his things, it was now mandatory that he make an appearance at his parent's party.

His black Armani suit hung lazily in the closet. He had hoped the next time he pulled it on would be to celebrate a very different kind of occasion. He retrieved it from the closet and laid it across the bed.

Taking a whiff of himself, he realized he reeked of sweat and wine. It was long past time for a shower and a heavy dose of sobering up.

He stripped off his t-shirt and jeans, discarding them on the bedroom floor and reached the bathroom with only his burgundy boxer briefs covering him. He turned the shower on to let the water heat up while he took a long look at himself in the mirror.

His usual stubble had turned into a full fledged crumb catcher.

*That will have to go,* he thought, and raised a pair of scissors to the coarse hair on his face.

The metal clinking of the scissors echoed around the bathroom as tiny particles of deep black hair fell into the sink below him. Once he was in a halfway decent state, he set the scissors down on the counter and peered into the mirror at his reflection, noticing for the first time how much he really had changed since the last time he had seen her. His brilliant blue eyes had turned to a dull gray, the circles below them a faint purple. He hoped they would be rejuvenated soon enough. On the bright side, his physique was still that of a Greek god, having replaced sex with exercise. His silky black hair was a bit longer, now teasing the tops of his ears and collar.

Stepping into the shower, he felt the falling water caress every inch of his body. He lathered himself up, letting the musky scent of the shower gel fill the air. His wet hair whipped lightly across the back of his neck as he thoroughly rinsed himself, before turning to the shower mirror to coat his cheeks with shaving gel. The razor stroked cautiously across his cheeks, savoring the cut of each hair. He felt slightly odd without his trademark stubble, but he was sure it would soon return.

He stepped out of the shower refreshed and feeling a few pounds lighter. Taking a deep breath, he let the remaining steam fill his lungs while he towel dried, and a moment later, he was slipping into a soft clean pair of black boxer briefs. It was almost an effortless routine as he slipped on his crisp white shirt, black pants, socks, and shoes. He had no problem adjusting the black tie around his neck or fastening his grandfather's diamond cufflinks at his cuffs. It's when his jacket was finally hugging his torso that the dance came to an abrupt halt.

He pulled a slip of paper from his pocket where Lily's simple words were scrolled across it in black ink.

*Ti do tuttu il mio amore.*

His Italian was rusty at best, but Lily's voice echoed it's meaning in his head.

*All of my love I give to you.*

Just remembering the way the words escaped her lips made his collar a little tighter.

He replaced the note in his pocket and took one last look in the mirror. The clean, somewhat sober man that stood there was prepared for anything.

He was anxious the entire drive to the Holt estate, possibly from the upcoming barrage of debutantes he knew he would have to wade through. Maybe it was due to the fact that he still wasn't quite sober enough to be driving. He kept his foot light on the pedal, watching for any speed traps.

He reached the house to find the driveway lined with every luxury car imaginable. It seemed like this was the one night of the year they were all brought out to shine. Ian wondered how many would actually make it home in one piece.

Ian parked his H2 a distance away so he wouldn't have a valet checking it. There was probably no chance in Hell he could walk in unnoticed, but that didn't mean he wasn't going to try.

His mother must have had her extra sensory radar tuned to her Ian frequency, as with only one foot in the door, he felt his mother, Marian, grasp his forearm. He felt like they walked aimlessly through a crowd of mindless socialites who all wanted their piece of Ian Holt.

Ian finally cajoled his mother into the den so he could explain his real motives for joining in on the New Year's fun.

"I might be going away for a while."

Marian became extremely agitated. "This is because of that girl, isn't it?" Ian tried to respond, but was cut off short. "I will not have any son of mine wasting his time on a woman he barely knows. Your career is just starting. You're on the verge of a huge recording contract, then possibly a tour after that. Is this woman really worth throwing it all away for?"

Ian looked at his mother with a crooked grin while she regained her composure. "Are you finished? Can I speak now?" Marian gave a pouting nod. "I've talked with one of Lily's friends and she's flying in tomorrow to meet me. She has a lead on where Lily might have gone after talking to her this morning."

"Now there's another woman you know nothing about, dragging you to God knows where to find the girl who ripped your heart from your chest!"

"Mother, Rebecca is an FBI agent who has far more resources than I do."

"FBI?" The vein in Marian's neck was throbbing in terror. "Is *this* Lily some sort of *fugitive* or something?"

"Of course not. Rebecca is just an old friend of Lily's from Portland."

"Oregon?" Marian shuddered. "Some lumberjack law woman traipsing cross country with my son? Absolutely not!"

"Mother, Lily is not a Hampton socialite, but that doesn't mean she's not worth looking for. I am sick of your ego based bigotry. I love Lily, and whether she's from Boston or Portland never mattered to me. I'm going after her."

"Good for you, son." Ian's father, Bradford Holt, appeared at the den's doorway, and walked over to take his wife's hand. "We've always taught him to go after what means most to him in this life. If this Lily completes him half as much as you complete me, she's got to be worth it."

Marian started to tear up as she embraced Bradford.

"Thanks, Dad."

"Just let us know if you get married so your mother knows when to put an announcement in the paper."

"I will." Marian left Bradford's arms for Ian's. "I'll be fine. There are just a few things I need to get from the guest house."

"Go on, son. Your mother has plenty of guests to attend to before this New Year's is over."

Ian shook his father's hand after he was released from his mother's rib crushing embrace. He began to sneak out the side door, before making a beeline for the guest house.

When he reached his destination, he realized nothing had been touched. He had forbidden his mother from gathering the staff to clean out the place and he was surprised she actually granted his request.

He walked into the closet, practically tripping over the mounds of untouched laundry and quickly filled his largest suitcase with thermals and sweaters. Heavy coats, jeans, thick pairs of socks, long underwear, and several pairs of boots were also crammed in before he finally zipped it shut.

He hauled the suitcase out into the bedroom and sat on the edge of the bed. Looking around the room, he couldn't help but think about what the following day would hold. Feeling hopeful for the first time in a long time, he smiled as one of his favorite memories crept up on him.

☙ ❦ ☙

Ian had only known Lily for six weeks, but somehow, it already felt like a lifetime. He stood in the doorway watching, as she towel dried her damp body; the caramel color of her bikini a stark contrast to her alabaster skin. Their midnight swim had put them in the mood for a much more exciting evening.

He stepped behind her, trailing a line of kisses across her shoulder. She let out a soft moan as her towel hit the floor. He continued the trail down her arm towards her elbow, her cool skin warmed with each kiss, causing a rosy blush to push to the surface. Before he could make it to his destination, she took her arm from his grasp and turned to face him, locking her arms behind his head. She teased her fingers through the wet hair that lay across the back of his neck. His hands moved to her waist, tempting themselves to pull at her bikini bottoms. He heard her sigh as her gaze fell to the floor, he brought his finger up underneath her chin.

"What is it?" He questioned as his kisses caressed her cheek.

Her chestnut eyes sparkled with flecks of golden hues as they met his in a moment of intimacy which he wasn't prepared for.

"I think I know where this is going."

"Is that alright with you? I'm...prepared, if that's what you're worried about."

A soft laugh escaped her perfect lips. "I know you are, the ever present Boy Scout."

"Too soon then?"

"No, no. It's just been a really long time. I don't have much experience with actual…love making."

"Love making?" He loved the way it sounded rolling off her tongue; so hesitant and innocent. "I'll take things slow, if that's what you want."

"I just don't want to disappoint you. I know how to be sexy and desirable, but when it comes down to, *it*, I'm such a novice."

"How many men have experienced this novice side of you?"

"Just one."

He knew she must have meant Ryan, the only other man she had ever admitted loving.

"What about you?" she asked, her fingers running lightly up and down the sides of his rib cage.

"Let's just say more than one and leave it at that." His coy grin seemed to make her uneasy and he had the feeling she knew it was many more than one. "Just know that I'm crazy in love with you. We don't have to go any further than this if you aren't completely sure."

"Really?"

"A first time together is a monumental occasion for us; I want it to be special. I hope this is my last first time." With that, her eyes sparkled with even more of a golden glow than before. Her eyes smiled, and filled with a playful glint.

"You know, now you're totally getting laid tonight." The grin swept back across his face as he leaned in to catch her lips.

Her sweet breath danced across his tongue as her lips parted to invite him in and he was unable to control the soft moan in the back of his throat as she intoxicated him with every flick of her tongue.

Her hands had slipped from the sides of his face, stroking his chest, circling his nipple. His fingers traveled from her hips up to the middle of her back. He jerked at the knot of her bikini top, releasing it instantly leaving the strings dangling at her sides. She pulled her lips from his, bringing her fingers to the remaining knot behind her neck. One more quick jerk and her top slid down her torso to hit the floor.

Lily pressed herself against him, gathering the heat that was brimming below his surface. Her finger pulled at the waistband of his swim trunks. He placed her hands on his hips and guided her to slowly pull them down. She traveled down with them, leaving soft, wet kisses down his chest, his stomach, until she came to rest upon his newly exposed hip. Her tongue lazily circled across the warm flesh. Her cool breath, so close to his center, sent waves of pleasure through his entire body. It was almost unbearable.

Ian took her wrist and pulled her back up to him, meeting her lips as he swept her onto the bed. She lay flat on her back as he positioned himself on top of her. "My turn." He wanted her to lay there and enjoy the ride. His tongue traveled from her mouth, down the hollow of her neck, across her collar bone, to her pert breast. Her pale pink nipple turned slightly rosier as his mouth gently caressed it. Her deep breathing led him to believe in her extreme concentration. He continued dragging his kisses down across her stomach, to her belly button and heard a small giggle escape her as his tongue slid to her hip. He took a breath and laid a soft, wet kiss where her pelvis met her thigh. She brought her leg up towards her chest as the giggles were now uncontrollable.

"Mmmm, I must have found the right spot." Ian smiled and went down to explore the site a little more.

"No, no. I can't take it anymore. No more teasing."

She lifted herself up, and started pulling at her bottoms. Ian took her hands and slid them off with her. They flew through the air, hitting the wall across the room. He brought himself up to her face to find her eyes were glowing like golden honey and her whole body felt much warmer after his exploration. He brought his lips to hers. She suddenly darted her tongue through his lips, searching the space that lay pass them. The ache they felt could no longer be kept at bay. His hips pressed flush with hers as he melted inside of her.

ଛ ᚹ ଶ

Ian lay back on his bed, praying that this memory would keep him going until he was able to melt with her once more.

# Chapter Four

## Tragic

ily's body had put a permanent dent into Renee's sofa and she was slowly becoming conscious enough to recall how and why she was there.

After every single person in town had bought her a drink, even she did not have the strength to walk, let alone drive home. As a vampire, she still felt the exhaustion brought on by a very long night. She had come to make the sofa in Renee's apartment above the bar a second home many nights since her return. She would surely have to buy Renee a new sofa after the ten hours of uninterrupted sleep and the effects brought upon it.

She curled her bare toes into the tan shag carpet, finding that her leg had crept off the side sometime in the wee hours of the morning. Somehow, it was soothing stroking it across the carpet that way.

"Lily? Lily, get up!" Renee shook her shoulders violently until Lily's eyes popped open.

"Was I snoring that loud?" Lily asked, slowly making it to an upright position.

"No. Damn girl, you scared the crap out of me. You weren't even breathing." Renee sighed, as she plopped down in the chair across from the sofa.

Lily just shrugged it off as her fingers felt the tangled knots that now inhabited what used to be her hair.

"You, young lady, had a pretty wild night last night."

"It did get a little rowdy after a while," Lily replied with a snort.

"I'll never forget the look on my father's face when you pulled him up on the bar and started singing. I didn't even know my dad knew how to carry a tune. You were brilliant, but he needs work."

"Must have been the whiskey we polished off. It's always a little more exciting when you've got some liquid courage on your side."

"Yep, the whiskey, the tequila shots, a few flaming Doctor Peppers, and don't forget all those blow jobs."

Lily picked up a pillow and threw it playfully at Renee. "You are terrible. Why did you let them buy all of those for me?"

"You only turn twenty-five once; I wanted it to be something to remember."

"Yep, only once." Lily rolled her eyes.

*If she only knew how many times I've said it was my twenty-fifth birthday.*

"I know you don't have any family here, but Dad and I...we consider you one of us; outsiders in this frozen wasteland."

"You're not really an outsider, Renee. You've lived here since you were fifteen."

"That's only ten years. I had fifteen years in California. You know, the California that's five hundred thousand miles from here? The one with ocean and beaches. Where tanned guys with rippling muscles surf all day and party all night. Tasting like salt water hours after the sun had gone down..."

Lily snapped her fingers in front of Renee's dazed face. "Come on, snap out of it. You've got a great life here. You have your business, your dad, and I'm sure your pick of eligible bachelors."

"My prospects are George, the fisherman who seems to always smell like the catch of the day, or Ivan."

"Which one is Ivan again?"

"The tall one, sandy blond, with the eye thing."

"Yes, that one's a keeper." Lily stood, did some unnecessary stretching along with a yawn for good measure. "So, what's on the agenda for today?"

"Clean up. We aren't opening till four, so we have a while."

"The least I can do is help. It was my party after all." Lily flipped her hair as she batted her eyelashes.

"I'm sure Dad's already down there, I can smell the coffee. I need to shower. I still have that Ivan smell all over me."

Lily sniffed the air around Renee. "That's what that awful smell is? I thought it was one of your new imposter body sprays."

"Hilarious, you are." Renee stuck out her tongue in mock disgust before making her way to the bathroom.

Lily had slept in her jeans and thermal. She found her socks and boots after a moment of searching and securely fastened them on her feet before jumping down the back stairs to the bar.

The bar was littered with glasses and bottles; they certainly had their work cut out for them.

"Erik?" she called. "I know you're down here. I can smell the...coffee." The smell made her gag a little, not one of her favorites.

As she made her way behind the bar and into the kitchen, the next few seconds slowed to a whisper as shock overtook her body.

A tall man stood above Erik's lifeless body. All she noticed was a long, black, woolen coat with jet black hair teasing about the collar, before covering her face with her hands.

"I'm afraid it's too late. There's no pulse." The man's melodious voice filled her with despair, but sparked a long dormant flame deep within her. Her breath caught in her throat as she let her mind deal with the possibility.

It felt like forever before she gained the courage to kneel down beside Erik. She heard no heartbeat. She felt no pulse. "There must be something..."

The man knelt down beside her. "I wish there was, but...feel. He's already cold."

Another man whom she had grown to love as a father was gone. Just another reason to distance herself from society all together.

The man brought his hand to Lily's face, sweeping her hair behind her ear, seeing her truly for the first time. "Lily," was all he said.

The next second, she turned to meet his gaze, but he was gone.

At that moment, Renee wandered in. She rushed to her father's side and her sobs were uncontrollable as she wept in Lily's arms.

ଅ ౪ ⱸ

"*Lily!*" His voice reverberated over and over in his mind as he felt his body thrash through space and time.

When everything became very still, he ventured to open his eyes. He was now seated in what had all the appearance of a coffee shop. Grinning enormously across from him was Peter. The man shook his head in disbelief as Peter rushed his fingers through his perfectly quaffed russet hair.

"What? No hello? How are you? Nothing?"

The man was by no means amused. "What just happened, Peter? She was right there. I touched her."

"Have some coffee. You're going to be here a while." Peter waved his hand in front of the man producing a cup of steaming hot coffee. "Or would you prefer cappuccino?" Another wave and Peter produced a cappuccino.

"I just want to know what's happening. Was it her? Could it really be her?"

Peter pulled out what looked to be a state of the art cell phone. "This might explain a few things."

"The Big Man's finally gone high tech, eh?"

"He's beginning to come around. Just take a look." Peter offered up the phone by sliding it over to the man. A video began to play on the small screen, Lily sitting in a train compartment, gazing at the countryside out the window.

"Do you remember this night?" Peter questioned, as he took a drink of his coffee.

"Of course, how could I forget? The first night of our honeymoon."

They stared at the video as the man saw himself enter the compartment.

ଧ ୴ ଷ

*Lily couldn't take her eyes off her new husband. She slowly took in all of his features, from his magnificent blue eyes that complemented his high cheek bones to his jet black hair that fell in perfect disarray to his shoulders. His muscular torso visible through his half unbuttoned shirt to the gold band that now had its place on his left hand.*

*"What is it?" He asked, as he brought her into his arms.*

*She laid her cheek against his bare chest as he kissed the top of her head. Her gaze turned to his eyes.*

*"I'm still getting used to all this. It seems as though we've been waiting forever. I'm not sure I can believe it's all real."*

*"It is, my sweet. I'm so sorry it took us so long to get here. Seven years."*

*"Might as well of been seventy," she sighed.*

*"I can't believe we wasted all that time, putting on that show for my parents."*

*"They were just looking out for the both of us. I don't think they ever imagined that we were what each other was looking for."*

*"I'm so glad I finally told my father how we felt about each other," he said, tightening his grip around her.*

*"I thought your mother would die of joy. I wish we would have known*

*how happy they'd be, it would have saved us a lot of lonely nights."*

"They weren't all lonely." He spread a few kisses across her jaw. "Those secret meetings in the familiar hours of the night…"

"I hadn't had a decent nights sleep in years until our wedding night."

"When we could finally sleep together."

"Together, forever," she smiled.

A sharp turn tossed them down onto the bed as they embraced.

They had been standing on the edge of temptation for so long, it had become an effortless dance when they joined together as one. It felt like the most natural thing in the world to explore each others bodies, devouring every inch of flesh. Their sweet symphony, so new, yet so familiar. Their bodies were perfectly matched to each other; their souls entangled in the winds of fate.

ଛ ᛦ ଛ

"Forever…" the man laughed. "Why are you showing this to me? Are you trying to torture me? I know what happens next."

"But you don't know what happened after that, to her." Peter pressed another button and brought up a new scene.

ଛ ᛦ ଛ

His arms were wrapped around her waist as she grasped the railing. They stood on the platform at the back of the moving train, watching the sunrise.

"I never want to forget this moment," he whispered in her ear.

"I never will, Ryan." She turned around to face him, but the train caused another jostle. She lost her grip on the railing and went over the side, her screams echoed in his mind as she fell. He reached out for her, but the events happened too quickly for him to interrupt. Her body hit the ground and rolled down a steep hill. The trees were thick in the forest the train was cutting through and at that moment, she was gone from his sight.

Her broken body came to rest at the edge of a riverbank, blood streaming from the wounds she had sustained during her fall. She lay unconscious and barely breathing.

A broad figure came running to her side. He swept her up into his arms and sped off like lighting.

He laid her to rest on his bed in his home in the forest. He wiped the blood trickling from her nose with his thumb before he brought it to his lips and tasted it. A split second later, her wrist was in his tight grasp. He brought it to his mouth, bore his teeth dripping with his venom, and sank *them into her soft flesh.*

*She cringed slightly at first as the venom entered her veins. He continued to drink – three swallows, four swallows, five... Eventually, he broke his grasp and placed her arm back at her side.*

*Her wounds began to heal as her face contorted from pain to pleasure.*

ʁ ℣ ♌

Ryan turned off the video and threw the device onto the floor. He stared out the window, now with even more questions than answers while Peter picked up what remained of the shattered phone at their feet.

"He turned her. That's why she's still alive?"

"Not alive exactly, but existing, yes. If he hadn't, she would have made it up there much sooner than you did."

"I would have lost her anyway?"

"Yes."

"But now, that was her; it was really her. Why, why did you take me away?"

"It's been a long time. Her existence is very different now. She's not the same woman you married."

"She sat there, weeping for that man. He was human. How did she do it?"

"Years of practice. Lily blends in quite well with modern society. She's actually one of the good guys."

"A vampire? One of the good guys?" Ryan asked, genuinely curious.

"She's one of three on the roster at The Manchester Group. She's done some great work; pulled us out of more than a few scrapes."

"Then why now? Why this way?"

Peter took a long look into Ryan's face. He saw the desperation crying out from every pore. "Lily and I have worked together over the years. She's had a fairly rough time of it. When I realized who you were to her, I put some plans in motion."

"Do I even want to know?"

"I made some arrangements for you to take some time off. I'm not sure how long I can keep everyone off your trail, but I think she really needs you now. I know you need her."

"You're going to let me go back, just like that?" Ryan asked skeptically.

"Just like that? The man she found you with, he had been like a father to her over the past couple of years. She's going to begin questioning what she is. You need to be there, if only for a little while, to give her a reason to keep fighting. You deserve to be together again. I just can't guarantee how long it will be for."

"When can I go back?"

"Soon."

## Chapter Five

## Symphony Of Darkness

The darkness of Renee's apartment was all consuming. Lily's existence had become so intertwined with the humans around her, that she was subjecting herself to the ultimate torture. She was tormented by the love she felt for those humans, who by all means should only be a source of sustenance. Yet, she couldn't let go.

Since her re-birth, she had only been close to two humans in which she had to mourn their passing. Erik had taken her in over the past few years and for some reason loved her like another daughter. His kind eyes and robust smile always reminded her of her own father. She allowed herself to become part of his family, knowing with every part of her, it was a tragedy waiting to happen.

The other, was a young mother named Anne. Just the thought of Anne's horrific death and the agonizing years that followed sent a painful wave of raw emotions through her entire being. Now, once again, she would have to deal with the painful loss of a human who got too close.

The events of the day had left both she and Renee exhausted. Lily had tucked Renee into bed and settled down on the now ruined sofa with a warm brandy. She had taken a few minutes to *run* home and get a few things. Her laptop was the one thing she was hoping would ease her night of restlessness.

She had found a new sofa online. Maybe a small token of a new sofa would help ease the pain of the loss of a father... Most likely not.

She went to check her e-mail and saw that she had updates from Manchester. Her secretary, or more aptly put, her back-up, Tess, made sure she didn't miss a moment of all the necessary gossip. It was the third such e-mail in a week. Endless stock reports from all over the world stuffed her inbox. Sifting through everything, she finally found one worthy of study – a video file from Becca.

She opened the file and anxiously waited as it buffered. Becca appeared on the screen, sitting in a familiar chair, in a familiar room.

"Hey you! I know we just talked this morning, but I wanted you to see my smiling face and wish you a happy birthday. I'd say it's another twenty-fifth this year, right?"

Becca knew her so well.

"I really wanted to send you a present. I found something perfect at that antique market you love so much. Problem is, I don't know where the hell you are!"

Becca paused to gather her thoughts.

"You know, if I try, I will find you. Why don't you just save us both some time, and me all the heartache and just let me know where you are. I know you are having a rough time right now, but that's what family is for. I'm here for you. I love you and I miss you terribly, so get off your ass and come home. I will find you, you know I can. I want to hear from you soon." Becca tilted her head with a pout. "I hope you had a wonderful birthday."

The clip ended and Lily let out a huge sigh. She knew Becca would find her, but right now, she couldn't bring her into the life she had made. Becca was the only person who knew almost everything there was to know about Lily. At times it was a tremendous relief to have her, although at others, it felt like she had placed an overwhelming burden on Becca. She felt selfish for having her in her life, but even the distance could not break the kind of bond the two of them shared.

Lily knew she needed to put Becca's mind at ease, so she queued up the web-cam and swept a stray piece of hair behind her ear as she began. She knew she wouldn't be able to hide her emotions from someone who knew her so well, so she wouldn't even try.

"Hey sweetie, I was afraid you were going to reach through the screen and grab me if I didn't respond soon. Stranger things have happened, you know?"

Lily looked down at her hands, hopelessly intertwined. Her eyes dark pools, not from hunger, but from emotion.

"You know me too well. It has been really rough here, especially today. I haven't had a day like this since the day your mother died."

Lily's breath caught in her throat.

"Someone here, who I'd become close to, passed away today. I had nothing to do with it, mind you. A heart attack. Now, I feel I'll be here even longer than I had ever expected. I've kind of found a new home away from home. It's sort of effortless here, but I know I can't exist in this symphony of darkness forever.

I do miss you. It's been way too long since we've seen each other. I will never forget how incredibly embarrassed I was when I looked into the audience and saw you in the crowd. I thought I was going to get the talking-to, but you were just supportive as always. If you could find me in Vegas, I know you could find me here. I need a little more time. Just know that I'm safe and I can always take care of myself.

I think the temptation would be too great if I came back now. You don't know how close I came to telling Ian everything. I wish I would have been able to see how he'd react. I wish you would have seen us in Boston, it was almost magical. I knew him for such a short time, but there was something so familiar about him. I felt so safe, too safe. I let down my guard and somehow fell in love, something I thought would never happen again. Not after Ryan.

I know it's been a long time and he's gone now, but I can't get him out of my head. I remember everything about the last night we spent together. I know you've heard the story a million times, so I won't bore you with it. I guess I just want that again. I had it, a little, with Ian. But even though I love him, I couldn't doom him to a life with me. It's bad enough that you've been stuck with me all these years. I hope it hasn't been too terrible for you."

She stroked her slender fingers through the hair that dangled past her shoulders. "There will be a funeral soon, in a few days I think. I'll be kind of caught up in that for a while. I promise, we'll see each other soon. I love you."

Lily blew a kiss before shutting off the web-cam. Dry sobs came hopelessly pouring out of her as she pressed the button to send the video on its way.

# Chapter Six

## Impressions

"Agent Swift, if you would please fasten your seat belt. We are about to make our final descent. Welcome to Boston."

Becca had stowed her things away and securely fastened her belt at least thirty minutes before the pilot had made his announcement. She was trying to work through the hundreds of scenarios swimming through her head. She was at last meeting Ian – Lily's Ian. Possibly the man that could give Lily the happiness she truly deserved.

How would Ian take the news?

Would he even believe her?

How much would he want to know?

Could she really pull this off?

Her nerves were visibly fraying. Boston was only the beginning of her journey. Would Ian be willing to go with her after he knew their secrets?

Becca's private plane landed at Logan International Airport without incident. The steward had her bags in the awaiting black sedan before she even stepped on the tarmac.

She settled comfortably into the back of the sedan while getting back in touch with the real world as she had kept her Blackberry off the entire flight. Turning it on might have been a mistake. She was instantly flooded with messages – her boss calling asking why she thought this was a good time to take an extended vacation, her partner calling confused… Then, a welcoming voice, Sam Fleming.

She listened carefully. "Becca, or should I say, Agent Swift. I was so pleased to get your message that you were on your way back to Boston. My office will be at your disposal during your stay. You can reach me day or night through the office, as always. Look forward to seeing you soon."

She saved Sam's message and went on to her e-mail. Lily popped up as the video began to play and Becca started to tear up at the thought of her mother. Lily had taken such good care of her then. She hoped that whoever was hurting from their loss now, Lily would be a comfort.

"If you could find me in Vegas, I know you can find me here." Lily's voice echoed through her ears, as the vision of Lily getting her G-string stuffed on the Vegas strip came to mind. She knew the girl couldn't have gone as long as she had with all that pent up sexual frustration. She knew Lily had just needed to get a little down and dirty, flush it out of her system. She also thought that if she'd had Lily's body, she would have done the same thing.

The tears were free flowing by the time she mentioned Ian's name. When Lily admitted how much she loved him, Becca was convinced she was doing the right thing.

Lily's devotion to Ian led to her painful admission about Ryan. She had told Becca the stories over and over about their secret romance and Becca thought of it as the most tragic fairytale she'd ever heard. If she could do anything to bring the fairytale back by making Ian a part of her life again, she would do it.

The butterflies in her stomach fluttered as the car pulled up to the town house. She had just opened her car door to find Ian there with a hand waiting to help her out.

"I thought you were going to call when you got in."

She placed her hand into his as she gracefully slid from the sedan to the sidewalk. The butterflies turned into an raging swarm as she finally met his eyes. She could feel the blood rush to her face, causing that oh so embarrassing rose colored glow.

She noticed the heather gray t-shirt that hugged his torso in all the right places and the faded blue jeans hung low on his hips. He must have been in the middle of something; it was a cold January day and he had neglected to slip any shoes on or a coat. His bare feet with perfect toes made her a little unsteady on her high heels.

"I got a little…distracted, sorry."

Becca's voice slightly faltered as she spoke. She wasn't really sure what to expect of the man who stood before her, looking her over. She was dressed in her most professional outfit and had added the heels instead of her usual flats to place herself at a more confident height.

Ian noticed her black pencil skirt below her tailored matching jacket. A hint of powder blue peaked above her jacket buttons, concealing it almost completely. Wisps of her auburn hair were falling around her face from the bun that rested at the back of her neck. He instantly felt like she was an old friend he was welcoming home from a long trip.

"No, it's fine, really. I'm so glad you're finally here. Is this all of it?" Ian asked, lifting the bags as the driver placed them beside him.

"Yes, but you don't have to..." She gave up as he ascended the front steps. She let her eyes drift to his firm biceps, bulging as he tightened his grip on the handles.

The driver drew her out of her daydream. "Let us know if you will need anything during your stay in Boston. Mr. Fleming has instructed me to have a car at your disposal at all times."

"Please relay to Mr. Fleming my sincere gratitude, and that I look forward to meeting with him again soon."

"Yes, ma'am."

The driver walked around the back of the sedan to the driver's seat. Ian was already back down the stairs before the driver had a chance to drive away.

"I hope you're hungry. When I need something else to do with my hands, I cook."

"I'm famished actually."

"Good." Ian led Becca into the house, straight to the kitchen.

An amazing aroma of tomatoes and fresh herbs teased her senses.

"I think you may have found my one weakness."

"Italian food, huh? I would have pegged you for a fish and chips kinda gal." Ian stirred his sauce causing fragrant waves to waft in Becca's direction.

"I love Italian food. I thought about becoming a chef for a while, even studied in Italy."

"What changed your mind?"

"I had a lust for violence. The FBI seemed like the safest choice." She felt her hair fall at the back of her neck. "Would you mind if I got cleaned up a little? It was a pretty long flight."

"Sure. I put your bags in the first room on the right." He pointed down the hallway.

"I'll only be a few minutes."

She slipped down the hall to the bedroom and found her suitcases lying on the end of the bed. She kicked off her shoes, and her feet immediately thanked her. She slipped off her jacket and skirt, before throwing them over a nearby chair. She stood in her powder blue tank top and underwear and pulled the band that was holding some of her hair in place. Her auburn waves fell far past her shoulders to caress her exposed backside.

She thought by Ian's attire, that casual was the way to go. She pulled out her favorite pair of jeans and slid into them and sighed at the instant comfort. She grabbed her navy hooded sweatshirt, slipping it over her arms, comforted by its soft cotton.

By the time she returned to the kitchen, Ian had dinner waiting.

"Come, sit."

He directed her to the kitchen table; a glass of red wine was already poured for her. She noticed the bottle sitting next to it.

"Lily's favorite."

"She left several bottles behind. I think she must have had stock in the vineyard or something."

*She does.* Becca smiled as he brought their plates to the table.

"I hope it's not too much. Just some sausage spinach ravioli with tomato cream sauce." He sat across from her awaiting her reaction.

"Wow, this is the closest thing I've had to a date in God knows how long." Becca smiled because it was so true.

"Don't tell me that you don't have a boyfriend, husband, or girlfriend to wait on you hand and foot."

"Uh, no. No boyfriend to speak of in three years, so definitely no husband. Never really thought of myself as having a girlfriend type, but maybe I just haven't met the right girl."

Ian smiled as he swallowed his first bite. "You were saying you had been distracted earlier."

"I thought I would try one more time to get through to Lily. I sent her a video message right after we talked last. She responded and I had to watch it to see if I could show it to you."

"I'd understand if you didn't want to."

"I do. There are just some things you won't understand and I'm going to have a lot to explain. Are you sure you're up to this?" Becca asked, taking a deep breath for good measure.

"I'm all ears. You can tell me anything."

"It's not all good. By the time I'm finished, you might want to give up on her all together."

"She's married?" Ian asked warily.

"No."

"She's a lesbian?"

"No."

"She's a Republican?"

Becca laughed. "No, I don't think she even votes."

"I don't see how anything you would say wouldn't be anything I haven't already thought of myself."

"I know she's really going to kill me for just being here," Becca sighed, taking a sip of her wine.

"You look like a woman who can protect herself."

"From drug dealers and corrupt politicians maybe, but Lily is a whole different story."

"Then we'll make your death a meaningful one. You're only looking out for her happiness, that will have to mean something."

"We'll see." Becca pulled her Blackberry out of her pocket. She cued up the video file and set the Blackberry down between them and held her breath as it began to play.

*"I haven't had a day like this since the day your mother died."*

Ian immediately paused the video and turned to Becca waiting on an answer.

"She was with my mom and I the day she died. If it weren't for Lily, I don't know how I would have made it."

"Can I ask, what happened?"

"A brain tumor; the one thing Lily couldn't fix. It all came on so sudden. By the time we found out, it was already too late. It was quick though, the doctors made her comfortable and in the end, I really don't think she suffered."

"God, I'm so sorry. I can't even imagine." Ian shook his head in disbelief.

Becca turned the video back on. Her breath caught in her chest as she heard Lily talk about Ian. His eyes smiled, glistening with unspent tears. Then she said his name – Ryan.

He knew very little about Lily's relationship with Ryan, but he could see that just the thought of his name was torture, as she explained how she just couldn't forget him.

The video came to an end with Lily's kiss to the camera and Ian turned to see tears streaming down Becca's face. He brushed the apple of her cheek with a dish towel. She laughed softly at the touch of his thumb across her tear stained cheek. It only made it worse.

"You really love her, don't you?" He asked, as he placed the towel in Becca's hand.

"She's my best friend. It's been really hard without her these past months."

"She said something about Vegas. You found her there?"

"After she left Portland last year, she turned up in Vegas. Only she could tell you why, but she ended up dancing at a club on the strip."

"Lily…a dancer?"

"More like a stripper. She never went any further than that with her customers. I think it was just something she had to do for herself. I don't know what happened, but she ended up leaving suddenly and came back here."

"Why wouldn't she tell me any of this? Why all the secrecy?"

Becca wiped a stray tear from her face then reached for the bottle of wine. She made sure both of their glasses were full. After drinking half of hers, she composed herself enough to go on.

"My mother worked for Lily. Lily had always tried to keep people at arms length, but my mom and I somehow got through to her. When my mom died, Lily was all I had. She took me in, even though she had no idea what she was doing. She helped me make the best out of my life."

"How long ago did this happen?"

"Take another drink before I tell you; it might help soften the blow." Ian reluctantly drank. "I was eight. I know you're thinking *'how is it even possible'*. This is the part where you should probably swallow before that wine comes spewing out."

Ian swallowed hard before following it up with another drink and swallow. "That would make her much older than you are. But, you look about the same age. How old is she?"

Becca opened her mouth but nothing escaped past her lips. She had never wanted to tell someone so badly the secret she had been holding inside for so many years.

Her silence was deafening and the wheels in Ian's head started to turn. Everything slowed and came into focus. The way her eyes changed color with her mood. Her aversion to the sun. Her reluctance to eat anything he offered her. Now, he'd realized she was much older than she said she was. He wiped his hand down his face, bringing his thumb across his chin.

"I didn't think people like that even existed."

"I think it's been easier for me to believe because I always knew things like Lily were out there."

"Things? You mean vampires. I can't even believe those words are coming out of my mouth."

"You heard her. She wanted to tell you," Becca implored.

"Tell me?"

"I told you that you might not want to go on looking after this."

He paused in deep thought, exhaling and inhaling as he carefully constructed his words.

"She raised you? A human. Isn't that some sort of oxymoron?"

"She doesn't feed on humans, only animals. That is the way she has always lived by."

Becca couldn't read Ian's emotions as his face blankly stared at the wall behind her.

"I can go." She got up to leave when he grabbed her wrist and pulled her back down to her chair.

"I'm still going after her. She can't get rid of me just because she's a vampire. I'm not letting her take the easy way out," Ian replied adamantly, as he finished his glass of wine and poured himself another. "She still loves me."

"Do you really know what you're getting into?"

"No, but you're going to tell me…everything you can."

Becca was hesitant at first, as she knew there was only so much she could tell him.

"She protected as much of her dark side as she could from me. She was an amazing mother, believe it or not. She's not the average vampire stereotype."

"So, you've met a lot of vampires?"

"Vampires, no. Thousands of other…beings you probably never thought existed either, but only two other vampires."

"Then, she's practically alone." The statement made him sad, sorry that she felt she couldn't let him in on the eternal burden she carried.

"She had another with her for many years. He was her sire, the man who turned her. All I really know about Martin is that he was killed about forty years ago."

"He was her…partner?"

"No, more like a father. He was in his forties when he was turned."

Ian was afraid of what he wanted to know next, but the jealousy was raging inside of him. He needed to know if he was competing with a memory.

"I need you to tell me about Ryan."

Becca swallowed hard, her throat dry and sore. She pulled the wine to her lips, pausing to stall as long as she could, letting the sweetness trail down the back of her throat. When his eyes met hers, she knew she couldn't hold out any longer.

"Lily moved from Boston to London after her parents died. She inherited their entire estate, which from what I hear, was quite vast. She sold almost everything off and went to stay with a friend of her father's and his family. Ryan was their eldest son, only a few months older than Lily. She and Ryan shared a special connection. His family became her new family and as a result, she was instantly seen as a daughter and Ryan's slightly younger sister by all of society. This caused a huge problem for their love affair."

"For years, his parents pushed suitors on the both of them. It had been almost seven years and they were still meeting in the garden or stables in the middle of the night. When Ryan's father demanded that he find a wife or he would find one for him, he professed his love for Lily. His parents rejoiced at the news – an unexpected turn of events – and she joined their family as Ryan's wife only two months later."

"His wife... All of these years, she had been faithful to him. Then I came along." A surge of uncontrollable guilt ran through him. He was her husband. Even though he was sure Ryan was dead and buried, Lily had broken a vow by being with him.

"How long were they married? Did they have any children of their own?"

"They only had three days. She was turned the second day of what was supposed to be their honeymoon."

Becca explained how Lily had fallen off the train and how Martin found her barely alive. Ian was silent and Becca feared for the thoughts flooding his mind.

Ian had no words. He felt awful and wonderful all at the same time. Awful for making her break a vow that she had obviously kept so close to her for decades, and wonderful for making him the one she would give it all up for.

"Did they ever find each other again?"

"She never said. I think it was all too painful for her. Even though she can't cry and doesn't seem to sleep much, some nights I swear she cried herself into unconsciousness," Becca sighed sadly.

"You took care of her as much as she took care of you, then?"

"I tried."

"What was it like, being raised by a vampire?" Ian asked, truly curious.

"Not as bad as you'd think. After mom died, we left Boston. If anyone asked, she was my older sister. We traveled, a lot, but we were never lonely. There was always someone we knew wherever we went. Rome, Paris, Prague, Tokyo, Beijing, New York, Green Bay..."

"Green Bay?"

"Lily loves the cold, plus she's a huge Packers fan. She was actually at the first Super Bowl," Becca laughed.

"When I decided to go into the FBI, she kept close. When I got assigned to Portland, she settled in nicely."

"I take it she's not really an investment banker then?"

"Not really. She's amazing with money, stocks and bonds, the whole thing, but she does something a little different for Manchester. She is one of those who uses her powers for good instead of evil."

"Powers?" His eyebrow raised above his sparkling blue iris. "What kind of powers?"

"You can't tell me that you have never felt them."

"With Lily, I've felt many things. I'm afraid you'll have to be a little more specific."

"There are the little things. Her strength, her speed, the keen sense of smell, and of course her amazingly unbelievable beauty."

"That, I noticed." He smiled with another sip.

"That's really all I'm able to tell you."

"Is it classified or something?"

"I'd guess you'd say that. Manchester has a very strict confidentiality policy," Becca stated, carefully edging around the topic.

"You don't work for them though, do you?"

"I used to. I had to get clearance to even tell you this much."

"So, she's some sort of superhero then and Manchester is her headquarters?" Ian asked, slightly disbelieving.

"That's about the size of it."

"Who's at the top, or is that classified too?"

"In Boston, it is Mr. Fleming. I got my clearance from him. I've explained everything to him and he's put the group at our disposal. They seem to want her back as much as I do, if not more. We have a meeting with him tomorrow."

"We, as in you and I?"

"You said you wanted in. You're not punking out on me now, are you?" Becca questioned, a small smile gracing her lips.

"Not a chance. You're stuck with me."

They went on for hours. The life she had led with Lily had him transfixed. Memories came pouring out of her, spilling effortlessly as the wine stroked the back of their throats. He was eager to know as much as he could about both of them.

Extremely light headed after they'd finished two bottles of wine, Ian went ahead and opened a third anyway. Becca fought to keep herself alert as she spoke even more softly with the occasional girly giggle. She learned exactly why Lily was so intoxicated by him and she felt more of that kind of pull herself.

In the middle of their conversation, they settled on the couch. They must have eventually passed out, as when she regained consciousness somewhere around four in the morning, Ian was cradling her in his arms. She hadn't felt so at ease with anyone so quickly in her lifetime. The warmth emanating from him was the ultimate comfort. She feared to move but she felt her fingers numb in their current state. She nuzzled at his chest and rested her hand there. Her movement stirred him, but he wrapped his arms tighter and pulled her even closer, and a few short moments later, she was lulled back into unconsciousness.

# Chapter Seven

## Scent Of You

After a trip home to shower and gather some more of her things in the early hours of the morning, Lily made her way back to Renee's. She wanted everything to be as perfect as it could be, as she was keenly aware that this day was going to be one of the most difficult days of Renee's life. She needed all of her energy focused on helping in whichever way she could.

A sign on the front door of the bar read, 'Closed until further notice'. Simple, without going into too much detail. The whole town already knew about the events of the previous day.

When she walked into the kitchen, it hit her like a tidal wave; the man. In all of her shock and disbelief, she really hadn't thought a thing about him. She smelled the air to see if she might be able to catch his lingering scent and the word that drifted into her mind to describe what filled her was Patchouli. An earthy, slightly musky scent she was all too familiar with.

She recalled how warm and soft the tip of his finger had been when he swept it across her chilled cheek. He must have known her, as she clearly remembered him saying her name. Then he was gone. She searched her mind for a possible answer, but didn't want to give into the possibility.

Peter, that was her answer. He must have been sent by Peter. Peter had helped her so many times deal with the most difficult of beings. He had been by her side the day Anne died and had promised to protect Anne's soul, carrying it to where it belonged, at peace.

She thought if vampires could have guardian angels, Peter was surely hers. Peter always had hope for Lily. He promised he would be there with her when it was her time to carry her soul to rest, but not until she finished what God had planned for her.

She couldn't ever really believe that God would send one of his angels to protect and watch over a vampire, but that is exactly what Peter did. He would show up when she needed him, and sometimes, even when she didn't. He was like the brother she never had. It gave her hope that one day, she might be able to experience a peace that God intended for her.

It was then she realized, the man had been an angel of death; there to help Erik to his place of eternal peace.

ଛ ᴡ ଜ

The weight lifted from Ryan's chest with every snow crushing step. Only mere feet from her door, he felt like his feet were no longer hitting the ground. He knew she wasn't there, but he was about to re-enter her world, finally.

With the sweep of his hand, the door clicked open. Her house was set miles away from any semblance of civilization. No one would ever know he was there, except her.

He stepped in, taking in the sight of the open area - living room, dining room, kitchen all laid out in front of him. Then the scent hit him – sweet red currant. It almost knocked him completely off his feet. He followed the scent to its source and found a candle that had recently been extinguished set on the stove.

*"She must have been here this morning."* Just the thought of her standing in the spot he currently occupied, blowing out the flame, sent a warm chill throughout his body.

As he snooped through her kitchen cabinets, he wondered just how much she might have missed food. Some of his fondest memories were of their time in the family kitchen. Helping Emily, their cook, with meals was just another excuse to spend time together. It didn't take Emily long to realize why they were there, as Ryan was a terrible cook. He never minded peeling the potatoes though, just to have Lily within reach. Emily became their Friar Tuck, so to speak. She'd often leave the most succulent concoctions waiting for them to enjoy during their late night rendezvous. He would never forget the taste of Emily's delectable apple pie on Lily's lips.

With only coffee mugs and wine glasses filling one cabinet, the others were filled with candles of every shape, size, and scent. Each fragrance held a powerful memory.

The Irish Cream, a recollection of his father's favorite after dinner treat, slipped shamelessly into his coffee. Roasted chestnuts for the time they tried to do it themselves in the formal fireplace with quite disastrous results. Rosewood for the tree that stood just outside her bedroom window. She had told him that Patchouli had always reminded her of him, the way he smelled after a long ride. Tucked in the back, a row of apple pie candles beckoned to be burned.

He placed one on the counter and lit the wick, and the aroma almost brought tears to his eyes. After all the time that had passed, he'd realized that she had never forgotten him. Every scent was a memory they had shared. He took solace in the thought that she kept them near to keep those memories alive.

He half expected some sort of blood waiting behind the refrigerator door, but instead he found dozens of bottles of red wine. Six of a Bordeaux Merlot, seven of a distinctly labeled Pinot Noir and eleven bottles of Cabernet Sauvignon. She had always loved the rich taste of the currants in each Cabernet they had tried. A new attribute he would add to the list of things he loved about his wife – an amazing wine connoisseur.

He noticed one had already been opened and didn't waste any time in finding a glass to pour it into. The glass went to his lips, taking in its bouquet. He let the rich sweetness pass his tongue, delicately dancing past his palate.

He held the glass between his fingers as he made his way over to her living room. He could picture her there, curled up with her favorite book on the enormous leather pillow, which he could only assume was her couch.

A flat screen TV with every amenity attached to it, was neatly packed into the cabinet beside the fireplace. A few games, several action movies, and a few more that showed the true romantic side of her, were scattered sporadically on a table beside the cabinet.

He brushed his fingers across the spines of the books compiled on the mantle. He pulled out a black, leather bound book wedged between two others. The date had him eager to find what may lie in its pages. He sunk deep into the couch as he opened the book to the first page. Her journal, he realized.

At first, he laughed at the picture of the girl called "Cinnamon". He remembered what a passion she had for dancing, but never thought of her dancing like that for him.

By the words set on the pages, she had enjoyed Las Vegas. She loved the freedom in the night, able to roam without being noticed in the crowds. She complained about having to hunt so far away from town to find anything better than an iguana, but she seemed happy all the same.

Almost twenty pages were filled with intricate details of her car, the McLaren SLR. From her description, it was one of the possessions she cherished most in this world. A guilty pleasure in which only she could enjoy the spoils.

He flipped further into its pages to find a picture of Lily, in the arms of another man. He froze when the caption below read "My Ian".

Realistically, he knew that over a hundred years had separated them and he had no right to deny her any happiness. It was inevitable that she would find love and comfort in the arms of another, and as he read on, he found that's exactly what she had found with Ian Holt. He *should* have been happy that she had found someone to love her the way she deserved, instead of being alone for over a century.

But undeniable relief surged through his system when he saw the words "He'll never be my Ryan, no matter how desperately I want him to be," and he immediately felt guilty.

An entry in October had him grasping at his chest; Ian had asked Lily to be his wife. But in the last entry, she explained why she thought it could never be.

*I love him, of course I do. It might not compare to what I felt for Ryan, but it doesn't make it any less real. He loves the idea of me that I have put in his mind but he can never know what I really am; no matter how much I want him to. I should have remembered how the physical side of love was never the most important part of a relationship. My memories of Ryan had always sustained me until I met Ian. Now that I've had to move on, they will be all I'll ever need until I can see my husband again. I have to believe in Peter's word to help me when it's my time. It's that hope that will help me survive.*

He slammed the book shut in anger.

"Peter, I should've known."

After their meeting in the coffee shop, he knew there was so much more he wasn't telling him.

He tucked the journal back in its place on the mantle, as everything needed to be kept in its place. He knew his scent would linger, but he didn't want to scare her by having anything disrupted.

He made his way to what he thought was her bedroom, but as he opened the door, he found it was so much more. Not just simply a bed, nightstand, and dresser, it was *her*. He grabbed her pillow, taking in her scent. Slightly fruity, surely her fragrant shampoo.

On her dresser was a jewelry box. Curious, he looked inside to find a diamond pendant, several pairs of jeweled earrings, and a locket. He opened the locket to find a picture of Lily and a little auburn haired girl. The tiny inscription on the back read "World's most unconventional mom. Love, Becca."

Lily, a mother? That couldn't be right. This sent him snooping further, pulling the trays out of the box to find a small black box tucked in the corner.

He opened the box to reveal a delicate gold wedding band. He had never suspected after so many years, she would still have the ring he gave her that day. His had been lost, he was sure, or handed down to another relative. This gave him an idea.

He went back to the kitchen with the ring securely on his pinky. He found a piece of paper and a pen and wrote a simple note. He placed the note with her wedding ring beside the candle he had just blown out before leaving the house with a smile.

## Chapter Eight

## Horizon

*T*he bell above the bar's front door dinged softly as it opened and closed quickly.

"Sorry, we're still closed," Lily called out from behind the bar.

"Even for an old friend?"

Lily looked up to see Peter dressed in a huge parka with fresh fallen snow weighing down his russet colored hair.

"It had to be Iceland again? You and cold weather..."

She immediately jumped over the counter and met him at the door.

In his best girly voice he gushed, "I know, I know. It's like, oh my God!"

The most elegant smile crossed her face as her arms surrounded him in a tight embrace. His hands went up to either side of her cheeks, stoking his fingertips across one side.

"I've missed you so much," she admitted.

He bent her head down to kiss her forehead. "I've missed you too," he replied, wrapping his arms around her waist, taking her in with his warmth.

"I love how you do that," she sighed, as her core started to slowly melt in his embrace.

"One of my many talents."

Renee came barreling down the back stairs to catch the two of them in their embrace.

"Oh, sorry. I thought..."

Lily and Peter walked over towards the bar where Renee had taken a seat.

"How about a drink?" Lily inquired.

"I could use something to warm me up a little more. How do you stand this weather? It's brutal." Peter stated, as took off his parka and set it across the bar.

"This is Peter, by the way. Peter, Renee. Renee, Peter." Peter stuck out his hand, which Renee accepted and shook.

"I heard about your loss. I'm deeply sorry."

"Thanks." Renee sat quietly as Lily poured three cups of coffee. Only a splash made it into Lily's cup, the rest was filled with Irish Cream. She topped the other two off and offered them to Renee and Peter.

"Still hate coffee, do ya?"

"Never quite got the taste for it." Lily grinned as she took a sip from her cup.

"So, are you two friends or something?" Renee asked after a sip, looking back and forth between them.

"Lily never told you about me?" Peter asked, raising his brow at Lily.

Lily just shrugged as she held her mug up to her lips. "It never came up."

"Oh, Lil…you never told your best friend about your only brother?"

"Brother? No, she didn't. I thought she only had a sister."

"I'm kinda the black sheep," Peter chimed. "I don't come around much, so she doesn't really claim me that often."

"So, you were just in the neighborhood and thought you'd stop by?" Renee asked.

"I'd heard what happened and I know how Lily is. She takes everything upon herself, so no one else has to. I thought I might give her a hand."

"That's sweet." Renee replied, blushing under the rim of her coffee cup.

"Is there anything else we need to do?" Lily asked, after sending an evil eye stare over to Peter.

"No, I think we pretty much covered it this afternoon. My mom's plane should be in tonight. She called after she landed at JFK. I'll have to go get her at the airport in Reykjavik. Actually, I should probably get going." Renee stood and grabbed her coat from behind the bar, wrapping it around herself. "It was nice to meet you Peter. I hope you'll be staying around for a while."

"I might be able to spare a couple of days."

"I'll call you when I get back then. You make sure and lock up before you head home."

"I will." Lily hugged Renee before she headed out the door.

Lily sat back down next to Peter. "Are you going to tell me why you're really here?"

He took another sip of his coffee, before lacing his fingers through hers.

"We need to talk."

"I've been good, I swear."

"I know, I've been watching."

"Sure you have. It still kinda creeps me out, the fact that you could be watching me at any time, any where."

"It's my job. Besides, someone needs to look out for you."

"Hey!" She punched him lightly on the shoulder. "I take care of myself just fine."

"Sure you can. Coming here, running away again..."

"I'm doing well here. I've got the perfect little house, some good friends and I've got a great job down at the gym."

"Teaching kickboxing to a bunch of horny teenage boys is not a career."

"It's a healthy way to act out aggression. Plus, they have an endless supply of mountain goats. I'm set."

"Mountain goats. Much better than coyote or iguana?"

"Saw that, did ya?"

"Yep."

"That's the creepy part."

A soft smile pressed into Peter's lips. "It was pretty interesting seeing you parade around in that little red outfit, if you could even call it that."

"That's not a very brotherly thought."

"I'm still a man, somewhere, deep down. I can't deny that you are and always have been an extremely beautiful woman."

Lily rolled her eyes.

"I know, things haven't been too wonderful lately, but I'm sorry to say, it's going to get worse before it gets any better."

"Worse?"

"I promise that you will have help and you'll be rewarded in the end."

"You're going to stick around then?"

"Not for long, but I'll pop back in if you need me to. You actually have a variety of things to help you and I wouldn't be surprised if there is something waiting for you at home right now."

"Some*thing* or some*one*?"

"Something for now. Just be prepared for anything, good or bad."

"That's all I get? Tell your boss I love how vague all your instructions seem to be," Lily replied dryly.

"He'll appreciate that, but I'm going rogue on this one."

"Breaking the rules? You really do care," she said, as she tossed her fingers through his still damp hair.

"You know I haven't forgotten my promise."

"Does this mean it's going to be soon?" She was excited at the thought of maybe being able to cross over, but terrified at the same time.

"In time, but I don't see it happening any time soon. Just go home and get some rest; you're going to need it."

"You're leaving then?"

"Duty calls, but I'll be back soon. I won't wait so long between visits next time." He brought his finger under her chin and pressed a chaste kiss to her lips before bringing her back into his arms.

Seconds later, she had been transported back to her own kitchen where she stood alone.

"He better have made sure everything was locked up."

She took a deep breath and took in the scent of fresh apple pie.

*I swear it was the red currant I was burning this morning.*

She looked to the stove top, where she noticed the apple pie candle sitting next to the red currant. Then she saw a note with her wedding ring.

She grabbed a hold of the counter to steady herself, suddenly feeling more than a little off balance. She picked up the ring to notice the extraordinarily familiar scroll on the note.

*Don't be afraid, my sweet. I'll be here with you soon.*

*R.*

She ran around frantically searching the house. His scent was everywhere. Is this who Peter had meant? She was sure; her Ryan had been there. The ache that consumed her body raged at the thought she might be able to hold her Ryan again. She took the pillow from her bed and wrapped herself around it; lying in the dark as she let the memories slip back into her mind as another seemingly endless waiting period began.

# Chapter Nine

## Secrets

ecca was startled awake by the vibration emanating from her left hip pocket. Her Blackberry had been turned to vibrate and was beckoning her to answer. She rose slowly, taking Ian's arm from around her and placing it on his chest.

"Hello?" she answered in hushed tones.

"Rebecca, I'm so glad I got a hold of you."

She sat herself down at the kitchen table, making sure Ian was still resting peacefully. "Sam. Sorry I didn't get back to you last night."

"No problem at all. I was just inquiring after Mr. Holt. Will he be joining us today?"

She noticed Ian had become conscious even after all her precautions and watched as he stretched up to his feet, sending her a smile as he saw she was on the phone. "Yes, he'll be there. How's your schedule today?"

"Barring any other catastrophes, I'm at your disposal."

"You don't have to do that you know. I think I can still find my way around that place – it's kind of hard to forget. You haven't restricted my clearance or anything have you?"

"No, you should be just fine. You meet Emma at reception and then come on up. I just wish that I was able to tell you where she was, but you know how tricky those blood oaths are. They don't make them with any loopholes."

Becca raised an eyebrow at his comment. "A blood oath? She must really not want to be found."

Ian came and sat across from her at the table, still stretching and yawning.

"I can't say much, but I *can* make sure that you're heading in the right direction. It's the least I can do after all you've done for us."

"Well, we just woke up, so we'll get dressed and head over." Ian nodded in agreement.

"I'll have a fresh pot of that tea you love waiting."

"You're too good to me."

"Only for you," he replied, and she could hear the smile in his voice.

"Be there soon."

"Looking forward to it."

Becca ended the call and looked up at Ian's exhausted expression. "Mr. Fleming," she stated, motioning to her phone.

"I got that much. So, what do I need to wear today?"

"Black on black – no tie. I think it'll make a statement."

"What am I trying to say?"

"Something like 'Yes, I'm human, but I've got powerful friends, so don't mess with me'."

His first smile of the day spread gloriously across his face. "I think I can handle that. Give me about ten minutes?"

"Good, that will give me just enough time with a few minutes to spare," she replied, and started towards the room she was supposed to sleep in.

"Do I hear a challenge?"

She turned back. "Are you up for it?"

"You're on."

He ran down the hall after her but she reached her room first, so he slowed. She hadn't realized that the door hadn't shut all the way, and as she stripped off her hoodie and tank top, Ian caught a glimpse of a large crescent shaped scar in the middle of Becca's back. Just the sight of it brought on a wave of pain and he wondered what she had done to receive it. Was it in the line of duty? Was it something much darker than that?

His mind was flooding with all the possibilities as he dressed and shaved. By the time he made it back to the kitchen, Becca was already dressed and seated back at the table. Her hair perfect, not a strand out of place as it flowed across her shoulders, and her royal blue shell top coupled with her black designer pant suit brought out her brilliant blue eyes.

She looked up at him and saw that he had fulfilled her request. He was wearing a black suit with a black button down shirt and no tie, leaving just the two top buttons open.

"Sorry to make you wait, I had to shave. It took me about an extra three minutes."

"It's okay. I called for the car, it's already waiting for us out front."

"You're some sort of amazing."

"Just keep remembering that," she said with a smile, as she led him out the door into the awaiting black sedan.

The car ride should have been uneventful, but Becca was a bundle of exposed nerves. Ian ended up trying to reassure her by taking her hand, and that just brought on a host of all new problems.

The feel of Ian's fingers intertwined with hers brought back a rush of feelings from the night before. The way his arms felt wrapped tightly around her as she slept was amazing, but it was odd that she would feel that way. Becca really never liked to be touched. She had stayed away from relationships for the past three years because she had been touched by so much violence in her lifetime. When it felt good, it scared her. Her thoughts drifted to Ian's hand caressing the skin at her hip. His fingers entangling her hair, his lips on hers...

"You ready? I think we're here."

Becca looked out the car window to notice they had already been driven under the Manchester building. A long tunnel housed the entrance to the high security wing. A black door at the end was only noticeable by the dim light cascading down from above.

Ian helped Becca out of the car and the driver was gone before they even made it to the door.

Becca found the hand scanner and laid her right hand upon it. The scan completed and the door opened to a large gray reception area.

The whole room was completely monotone except for the spiky haired blonde who sat behind the desk.

"Good morning, Emma," Becca said to the receptionist, as she pulled out her security badge. She swiped it across the desk and Emma became animated, as her blonde spikes turned to a lovely shade of red.

"Welcome to The Manchester Group, Agent Swift. Please standby for retinal verification."

Emma stood and Ian watched on as Emma's eyes sent a brilliant red light floating across Becca's.

"Retinal scan confirmed, Agent Rebecca Swift. Access granted. Enter the elevator to your left which will take you directly to Mr. Fleming's office. Have a nice day." Emma returned to her seated position as Ian and Becca made their way to the open elevator.

"So, she's an android?" Ian whispered as they entered.

"I guess you'd say that." The doors closed in front of them and the elevator began to rise. "She's more like a super intelligent security system. I've only seen her skills in a demonstration, but she is definitely one of the fiercest things I've ever seen. You wouldn't want to come across her in a dark alley."

"I'll remember that for next time."

"You're already thinking of a trip back?"

"It doesn't seem that bad so far."

"Let's just see how today goes."

"Is there anything I should be worried about?" Ian asked hesitantly.

"Just follow my lead and you should be fine."

The elevator opened to an empty office. As Becca stepped into the room she looked over the monochromatic walls to a black mahogany desk settled just in front of a wall of windows. The desk chair swiveled around to reveal Sam Fleming.

"Rebecca." He rose from his chair as she made her way to him. She rushed into his arms, and was immediately enveloped by his warm embrace. "Let me take a look at you," he smiled as he pulled back.

Becca noticed that he hadn't changed at all in the years since she last saw him. He was still just as tall and lean, with salt and pepper hair cropped short above his ears. His electric blue shirt resting under his black suit emphasized the rim of blue that surrounded his unusually large black pupils.

"Much too long between visits." He pulled her back in and placed a kiss into her hair.

"Way too long," she agreed and pulled back to beckon Ian to join them. "This...is Ian Holt."

"Very good to finally meet you," Sam stated, as he took Ian's hand in a vigorous shake. "I've heard so much about you."

"Sorry I can't say the same." Ian took his hand back from Sam's, unconsciously placing it on the small of Becca's back.

"Where do we start, Mr. Fleming?" Becca asked, slightly blushing from Ian's contact.

"You know you can call me Sam. I'm not your boss anymore."

"Where do we start then, Sam?" Becca repeated with a smile.

"The vault. She has had me sending her items occasionally so I've become pretty familiar with her things. I think you'll find your answer in there."

"Are all her journals there?"

"All but this last year which she has with her. I think there's something down there she wouldn't mind letting you borrow." Becca's eyes lit up. "That way you won't need the driver anymore. At least while you're in town."

"The McLaren? She hasn't even let me touch it, let alone drive it. Are you sure?" Becca was eager for an affirmative answer, as she'd always dreamed about tearing down the highway in the car of her dreams.

"If anything was to happen to her, it's always been her wish for you to have everything. Since she's indisposed, I can't see why not."

She jumped up and put her arms around him like she was a child who was just given a pony. "Thank you so much."

Ian stood smiling and shaking his head in disbelief.

"What?" Becca asked as she removed herself from Sam.

"I've just never seen any other woman besides Lily get so excited by a car. You really are her daughter."

"Lily did a fine job with this one. A struggle, but Lily never gave up."

"I could be a handful. Especially for that year in Rome," Becca replied as she rolled her eyes.

"Let's not revisit that disaster. I'm sure Ian's excited to see the rest of the place. I can give you a tour?"

"I'd like that."

The three of them made their way back to the elevator and went down three floors before stopping. The doors opened and Sam led them down a busy corridor. Many took notice of the three of them walking through, as they stopped for a moment for a formal greeting towards their branch president, before hurriedly returning to whatever task was at hand.

Ian thought not many of them looked very out of the ordinary. Some had a slightly different color tinge to their skin or unusually large pupils, but there were no horns or scales, no third arms or eyes. Maybe this wouldn't be so bad after all.

They headed towards a desk at the end of the hall where they found a lanky brunette behind the desk and Becca stepped in front of Sam to approach her.

"Guess they still allow filthy Crantorie demons in here?" Becca glared down at the woman as their eyes met.

"Security must be slipping if they've started letting traitorous leeches back in this place," the brunette replied icily. The glares turned into fits of laughter as the brunette came around the front of the desk and pulled Becca into a warm hug.

"So glad you finally made it back."

Becca pulled back. "You look amazing, Tess."

"I've had a little work done. Had that horn removed finally."

"Looks good." She turned to her companions and pulled Ian next to her. "Tess, this is Ian."

Tess brought him into a bear hug, shocking him to say the least. "I'm so glad you're here. I'm glad you finally know everything," Tess said genuinely as she released him, but not before letting her fingers trace circles across his lapel.

Becca pulled him away from her. "Manners, Tess. It's not nice to molest the visitors their first time out."

Tess bit her lower lip and dipped her eyes. "Sorry." Becca was obviously not the only one affected by Ian's aura.

"It's fine really. Glad to finally put a face to the voice."

Sam finally spoke up. "Is your boss in?"

"Yep, just finishing up a call to Athens."

"What poor guy is stuck with you now?"

"You didn't tell her?" Tess questioned Sam.

"I thought it would be a nice surprise," Sam replied, as he opened the door for Becca and Ian to go through.

As Becca saw the tall sandy blond standing with his back to them looking out his window, her face went completely pale. She turned back to try to run, but Sam had already closed the door behind them. It was too late, as he already knew they were there. Her terrified eyes glistened with unspent tears.

Ian wiped the tears away with his thumb before they had a chance to fall. "What's wrong?"

"Whatever you do, don't let go of me and don't let him touch me. Please?" she whispered, as she took his hand in hers.

"Sure. Anything," he replied with a nod, as she turned and plastered an incredulous smile across her face.

"It's been a long time." His voice hit her like a freight train, her chest throbbing in that all too familiar pain. She squeezed Ian's hand as the man made his way towards them.

"Just giving them a little tour. It's not often that she makes it back here," Sam stated as he eyed Becca forward. Becca just continued to smile, unmoving. "This is Ian Holt."

"Abe North. Nice to meet you," Abe stated, as he offered his hand to Ian.

Becca batted Ian's hand down when he reached to shake. "I don't think that's a good idea."

"Rebecca, let's be civil," Sam chastised as he turned to address Ian. "These two have a long history, you know."

"Really?" Ian eyed Becca. "I hadn't heard."

"Thought these two would be together for the long haul."

"Things don't always turn out the way you plan." Becca pressed her lips firmly together.

"I never really got to explain how..."

"I don't need to hear any empty apologies from you now," she stated, effectively cutting him off as she moved even closer to Ian.

"I never meant to..." Abe's eyes were consumed with guilt. "Everything's all right now, then? You're healed?"

Becca's free hand made its way around to the middle of her back where her scar ached just at the mention of it. "It took a while, but I'm fine now."

Ian turned to see the spot she was referring to. He felt an unfamiliar rage well up inside him as he whispered to Becca, "He did that to you?" She met his gaze, confused. He still hadn't broached the subject of him glimpsing her bare back as she was changing. He leaned into her ear. "I saw it earlier."

She mouthed the words, "I'm sorry. I never meant..."

"No. No." Ian pulled her into his arms. Her hands rested on his chest, her head at his shoulder. He lightly ran his fingers across where the scar lay beneath the layers of fabric. "Let's see if we can take care of this." Ian rested his forehead against hers. If his touch didn't feel so calming, being this close to anyone would terrify her. He lifted her chin up with his index finger, placing a soft kiss upon her forehead. Ian turned, slipping his arm securely around her waist.

Devastation swept across Abe's face as realization set in. "I had no idea you were with someone."

Sam opened up his mouth to refute the statement, but Ian spoke before first. "I would hope you would be man enough to be happy for us. I guess I should thank you, actually."

"For what?" Abe's voice was filled with nervous confusion.

"If the two of you had stayed together, I never would have gotten the chance to make her my wife." Ian's brilliant blue eyes reflected the gratitude in hers.

"The two of you are already married?" Abe looked like he was on the verge of tears as the words escaped his lips. The pain was almost excruciating.

"Not yet," Becca perked up. "Soon though. You'll understand if we don't include you on the guest list..."

Abe swallowed hard.

"I think we'd like to move on now, if that's all right Sam." Ian stated, as he pulled Becca towards the door, his hand still firmly at her waist.

"Of course," Sam replied, still reeling from the events that just unfolded before him. Becca and Ian went back through the door and waited at Tess' desk as Sam lingered. "I want a full report on the Athens situation and I expect you'll come to my office when I call."

"Yes, sir."

Sam closed the door as Abe caught one last look at Becca with her arm around her new fiancé.

"Rebecca, I can't tell you how sorry I am. I had no idea," Sam stated sincerely, as he caressed her shoulder.

"It's fine. I knew we would have to see each other again someday; I was just caught a little off guard. I thought he was still in London."

"When Lily left, we needed someone to fill in. He was available and willing to come back to the States. He'd been so devastated when he left Portland that I thought it might be a good change for him."

"Glad to hear he still feels guilty. Thanks for the save in there, I almost believed you." She smiled at Ian who was still holding her close at his side.

"He believed. That's all that matters." Ian squeezed at her waist before releasing her.

"On with the tour then." Sam led them to another set of elevators.

"Why don't we just go down to the vault? You don't mind, do you?"

Ian turned to Becca. "I think the sooner we get started the easier it will be for you. Maybe you'll cheer up at the sight of your new car."

That brought a smile back to her pale pink lips. "I had almost forgotten."

Sam took them through a maze of offices and hallways. Six different sets of elevators later, they reached the vault floor.

An endless deep space filled with boxes, creates, and side vaults. They walked in anxious silence for almost fifteen minutes before Sam stopped in front of a large side vault and keyed in a twenty digit combination into the key pad. When he completed his task, a green light flashed as the enormous, thick metal door lifted. Slowly, the McLaren came into view, just inches inside of the vault. Becca made her way inside and lightly ghosted her finger across the smooth body from bumper to bumper.

"I never thought I'd see it again." Becca sighed, resting her hand on the driver's side door.

"Her," Ian corrected. Becca turned to him with a look of confusion. "Lily always said this car was like her baby, her little girl."

Becca nodded in agreement.

"The journals are right over there. I'd say you'd be safe staying in the last ten years." Sam went over and opened a box behind the car.

"You don't know how much this means to me," Ian shook Sam's hand. "To us."

"If you can bring Lily back without any bloodshed, it'll be worth it."

Becca took a journal from the box. "I wonder..." Becca flipped through the journal to find a picture of her and Lily. "This was on her birthday that year. We were in New York City, in a suite we had above Time Square. We drank Champagne all night."

"I'll leave you two with your memories. Just call me when you're ready to take your new little girl home."

Becca pecked Sam on the cheek. "Thanks." Sam squeezed her hand before leaving the vault. She turned back to see Ian flipping through the journal she just had open. "We had so much fun. It was an amazing trip."

"Just you and her?"

Becca dropped her eyes. "No, Abe was with us."

"Oh. You want to talk about it?"

"We'll have time for that later. Let's get started with these." She picked up two thousand – three and two thousand – four. "She went on an extended trip in two thousand – nine, maybe start there."

He flipped it open to find a picture of a little house covered in snow. The caption below read 'my Icelandic getaway'.

"Iceland?" they said in unison, as they dug further into the journal. They read about her friends Renee and Erik and how she had bought the house as a getaway for some of the winter months. She loved the small town, the cold, and the solitude, but she missed her daughter.

Lily spent entire entries detailing her relationship with Becca. The tears threatened to fall several times, but Becca managed to keep them at bay.

"Could it really be this easy?" Becca questioned, as she continued to flip through the journal.

"Easy? I don't know about you, but the past two months have been hell for me."

"Sorry, I didn't mean... So, you up for an Icelandic adventure?"

"When can we leave?"

# Chapter Ten

## Gideon

The elevator dinged bringing Sam's attention to the opening doors. Abe slowly stepped out as Sam eyed him until he was standing at the edge of his desk. He set the file he'd been compiling on the Athens transaction on the desk.

"Sit." Sam gritted through his teeth. Abe complied, falling back into the chair behind him, knowing he was about to confess his most monstrous sins.

"I was always under the impression that you and Becca parted on friendly terms. Imagine my surprise when I find out just this morning that this was not the case. We've known each other for a long while you and me, Abaddon. I would expect nothing less than the truth."

"It's a long story…"

Sam's forehead creased at his impatience.

"I'm sorry, sir."

Abe began to recount his life with Becca. It had been three years, but the pain still haunted his fragile soul. Never in the hundreds of years he'd been walking the earth had he ever felt love. Becca was the exception. He had finally found meaning to his existence in the form of one perfect woman.

Her long auburn locks, sparkling blue eyes, her heart shaped lips, the curve of her thighs, all perfect in his eyes. He knew she had never seen herself as beautiful, being brought up beside the magnificent beauty of a vampire, but Abe never looked twice at Lily. All he saw was what his heart longed for, a soul mate. It was that love he gave to her body and soul that had almost destroyed her.

Abe was a delivery system of sorts, known only as a shadow walker. Things would pop up in the wrong place and he would transfer them or remove them completely. Demons, sometimes prisoners of war, he listened to a higher call and followed His instructions. With one touch, he could pull someone into the shadows, transporting them to any point in the universe. Could be heaven, could be hell, could even be New Jersey...

His main assignment for over a hundred years had been with The Manchester Group. A liaison, of sorts, with them and the powers that be, more commonly known as PTB. It was only when he met Becca that he began using his powers for anything other than what he was called to do. At a moments notice, they would be dinning in Paris, walking the beaches of Cancun, or shopping on the streets of Milan. Anything to show her what magnificent glory she had brought to his existence.

"Do you remember when she was assigned to The Monitor's task force?"

Sam nodded, as the recollection of her most terrifying case came sweeping to the corners of his mind. "Even we couldn't find him."

"She worked day and night, going through all the proper channels while I spent all that time going through the improper ones. I knew I had to find him once he singled her out, taunting her, but I knew I needed help. So I went to the one nobody would ever dream of teaming up with; Gideon."

Sam slammed his fist against his desk causing a large crater to appear. He carefully picked out the splinters as he tried to control his anger. "Gideon has been banished for decades. Why would you ever imagine he could help?"

"I knew he had resources I didn't. I thought he might be the only one who could help me save her. Turns out, he was the one she needed saving from. Gideon *was* The Monitor."

"And you led her straight to him?"

"I needed his visions to tell me how to find the psychopath. Then, he insisted on seeing Becca, saying only she could bring his purest visions to light."

"Then, what happened? I never heard a word of this."

"He held both of us for weeks and I remember hardly any of it. When I finally got us out of there, Becca was terrified at the sight of me. That's when I transferred to London. Lily assured me she would take care of her. Now, I guess she has that *Ian* to take care of her."

"He's only human though; I don't know if he's the right fit for her." His head dropped into his hands, then winched when he hit the spot where the biggest splinter had been.

"She seems quite attached to him, and the way he looks at her...I can hardly blame him."

Sam's secretary buzzed his phone. "Agent Swift on line three."

Sam picked up the phone with his good hand. "Yes, Becca...Wonderful, I'll meet you down there." He gently slid the phone back down and raised his eyes to meet Abe's. "We will deal with all of this when I get back."

Abe adjusted himself in his chair. "You're going with them...to find Lily?"

"I'm not letting her out of my sight."

ଧ ᐻ ଧ

"Sam's on his way down," Becca said, shoving her phone back in her pocket as she sat in the driver's seat of the McLaren. "Sorry, baby, looks like it wasn't meant to be this trip. I promise I won't leave you here for long." She stroked her slender fingers across the steering wheel as Ian started to chuckle in the passenger's seat. She turned to give him a stern glare as she pursed her lips.

"She's not even yours and you're treating her like your baby too."

"Hey, a lot of hours went into researching this car. Lily and I hand picked it. It's practically one of a kind with all of the extras it has on it."

"So, if you love cars as much as Lily, where's your McLaren?"

She brought the corner of her mouth up in a sweet smile. "I needed more of a company car. The McLaren is a little ostentatious for an FBI agent, so I drive a Saturn. What about you?"

"A Hummer – it just seemed like the right fit. Lily would even change my oil when I needed it."

"She taught me all that stuff too. I never had a dad to teach me about cars, so I learned everything from Lily."

"I have a father, but we never spent any amount of time working on cars. I was lucky if I got him to come to one of my football games."

Her brow creased in confusion. "I had you pegged as more of the baseball type."

"I was a kicker and a punter, before my mother realized I got tackled just as much as any of the other guys. She was afraid I would break my hands, so that was the end of my glorious football career. I even gave up a scholarship to Northwestern."

"Are you ever sorry you focused on your music instead?"

"Never," he replied firmly, his eyes lighting up at the thought of stroking his fingers across the keys. "I love it, but more than that, I crave it. The melodies, the feel of the ivory beneath my fingertips, the perfect last note..."

Becca's awe was apparent as she pressed her lips into a soft smile. "You talk about your music the way I talk about cars."

Ian nodded. "I guess we each have our own instruments, so to speak."

"How much withdrawal am I going to have to deal with?"

"As long as I have my iPod, I think I'll be alright." Ian tapped his fingers against his knees as he searched for how to bring up the subject he'd been wondering about for hours. "Truth or dare?"

"What?" Becca asked, practically laughing out the syllable. "This is really not the place to be doing any kind of dare."

"Truth it is then."

She twisted in her seat to meet his stare. "What do you want to know?"

He wiped his hand across his brow, preparing to ask the question. Any way he phrased it, he had a feeling it wouldn't come out right. He knew Abe had something to do with what he had seen on her back that morning, and he wanted to know why.

"I think if I'm going to be your fiancé for that Abe guy's benefit, I should at least know why."

She nodded as she dipped her head down. She had hardly ever talked about what had happened except with Lily; Sam hadn't even known. She felt the heat rise to her cheeks at the thought of those last weeks with Abe. Her palms got clammy, her pulse started to race. She took a deep breath before launching into what was sure to be a very long explanation.

"As you probably noticed, Abe's not exactly human."

"It's the eyes." He nodded as he blinked overtly.

"I met Abe while he and Lily were working at Manchester. I knew, with our obvious differences, it would never end well, but I never imagined..." She took a long, deep breath. "Abe is a shadow walker. He can pull you into his shadow and transport you anywhere."

"Hence, the not touching thing?"

"Exactly," she replied, trying to figure out where to start. At the beginning of the end, she guessed. "It all went to hell when I got assigned to 'The Monitor's' task force a little over three years ago."

"You were going after *that* guy? The one who burns his victims?" The vision of the scar on her back came blaring in his mind. A crescent shaped burn put there by a serial killer.

"Yes, much to Abe's disappointment. He became extremely overprotective and went to the ends of the earth trying to find any being that would be able to help us find the mad man. Abe has visions too. They work differently and for some reason were being blocked when he tried to use them for the case. He did find someone else to help eventually – Gideon.

Gideon had the power of foresight and was able to possess almost any living thing. He had been banished decades ago, but Abe assured me that Gideon had visions of The Monitor. We went to meet Gideon, only to find that the truth was…Gideon *was* The Monitor."

Ian nodded as he realized why The Monitor had never been caught. "He was possessing people to do his killing for him."

"He ended up torturing us for weeks. His favorite way to torture me was through Abe. Gideon would take over Abe's body and beat me into unconsciousness, but I wouldn't break. He'd burn me just like the rest of his victims and still, I didn't break. One morning, he strapped me down to a table with leather straps. I was so weak at that point I could barley move, but I promised myself that I would never let him break me. That's when Gideon came to me as Abe for the last time. He ripped the clothes from my body and crawled on top of me. He raped me as Abe and I couldn't even cry out for the real Abe lost inside of him."

It was all too horrible to imagine and Ian took Becca's hand as a tear ran down her cheek.

"That's where he made his mistake. He tossed Abe's body aside and returned to his own, deciding that he wanted *his* body inside of me, not just his mind. Somehow, Abe was able to gather enough strength to rip him off of me and we disappeared."

"A few days later, I woke up in a hospital in Portland with Abe holding my hand. At first I wasn't sure it was really Abe, but even when I realized it *was* him, I still couldn't stand the sight of him. I knew he wasn't Gideon, but I still blamed him for taking me there in the first place. All I could see was his fingers ripping at my flesh, feel the hot iron burning the spot on my back. When I walked into his office this morning, it all just came flooding back."

Ian reached to wipe a tear from her cheek, but she grabbed the door handle and jumped out. She was pacing in front of the car when he tried to approach, her breathing heavy as she began to cry. She couldn't stand anymore. Ian caught her and set her down by the wall as the sobs overtook her body.

"Hell of a time to have a panic attack," she sobbed, slowing her breathing in an attempt to calm herself.

"No, no, it's fine. Tell me what I can do. I'll do anything. Anything you want."

"It's just…he's still out there. He could get to me through anybody."

"I can't even imagine how you must feel." He couldn't really. He had never known pain or loss like Becca had. The last months of his life longing for Lily were nothing compared to what Becca had suffered through.

Becca rose quickly as she heard footsteps approaching them. She put her hand on her side arm as she took a defensive stance, shoulders squared, head up, in front of Ian.

"You both ready? The jet is fueled and ready to go."

Her defenses rested as she threw her arms around Sam's broad shoulders. "Did I miss something?"

"No, just a lot of memories in here," Becca replied, as she released him from her embrace and moved to gather the things she wanted, as Sam noticed a visibly shaken Ian.

"Becca and I just need to get our gear from my place then we'll be ready to go."

"I'll get my things and meet you at the plane. I have the driver waiting."

"You're coming with us?"

Sam brought Becca back into his protective arms. "I know I can't tell you where she is, but there's nothing against me tagging along while you find her. Plus, I just got you back," Sam responded, as he kissed her forehead. "You're not going anywhere without me."

"You sure? I have a feeling January can be brutal in Iceland." Becca pulled away from him, letting her fingers slip through his.

"I think I can handle a little cold weather."

Sam wrapped his arm around Becca's waist as they exited the vault. Ian picked up a few more things before Sam keyed in the same twenty digits and closed the vault. They walked away from the vault as Abe stepped away from the shadows.

"Looks like I'll be making a trip to Iceland." Abe straightened his coat and tie before disappearing into nothingness.

## Chapter Eleven

## Forever Found

"You know you don't work here, right?" Renee said, as she came around the bar to where Lily was wiping it down.

"I'm just trying to help." She put the rag down and turned to face Renee.

"I know." Renee wrapped her arms around Lily. "I'm fine, for now anyway." Renee pulled back, her arms still around Lily. "You go. Find that gorgeous brother of yours and have some family bonding time."

"Peter, right. He'll be working on something, I'm sure. I'll catch up with him eventually."

"Did he ever tell you when he was going to leave you that surprise?"

Lily shook her head. "No, not yet."

Lily trusted Peter, implicitly. She just didn't know what he was up to. If anyone could bring Ryan back to her, it would be Peter. But, why the note? Why the candle? Why not just find her and take her in his arms?

Lily picked up her coat and slipped it over her shoulders, before grabbing the stocking cap from her pocket. She shoved it on her head and whipped her crimson scarf around her neck. "I'll check on you later."

"Thanks for today. I don't know how I would have made it through the funeral without you."

Lily took Renee's hand. "Call me, really. If you need anything."

"I will."

With that, Lily headed for the door and into her awaiting Jeep.

Thoughts of Ryan were consuming her on the drive. She felt like she was going to crawl out of her skin. She needed to run, far and fast. The daylight was wavering on the horizon, but she couldn't stand the feeling anymore – she had to get out. She parked the Jeep at the edge of her usual hunting ground and stepped out into the fading light, almost every inch of her covered in fabric.

She took off at full speed into the forest. Her clothes were restraining. She wanted the feel of the wind on her face, it ripping through every strand of her chestnut locks. She tore the stocking cap from her head and the crimson scarf flew from her neck in one swift motion. She could feel her skin come to life in the soft sunlight. A golden glow streaking through the trees.

She ran until she reached a clearing next to the frozen riverbank. She sat at the edge, slightly exhausted, her lungs taking in each unnecessary breath. Her face illuminated in a golden glow of the waning sunlight, now only inches above the horizon.

She heard a sound from behind her at the edge of the tree line. She almost turned to see what was intruding on the perfect sunset, when the amazing scent of Patchouli hit her nostrils. If she had a heartbeat, that would have been the moment it would have started racing.

The anticipation had been torture for him. He couldn't stand to be away from her for a second longer. After watching her for only a day, he had fallen in love with her all over again. He had no idea what to say or what to do, he just had to have her and let her know he was still hers, forever.

He was only steps behind her. He knew she had heard him approaching, but she didn't turn to face him. Her head just dipped down to her side then back to straight in front of her. He crouched down behind her, knowing she was waiting for him to touch her.

"Wait, please?" she asked. The glorious pitch of those words resonated throughout his entire being.

"Forever, my sweet."

Her breathing became heavy and uneven as a million different possibilities for that moment came flooding through her mind. She wanted to turn and take him in her arms, never letting go. She had no idea how or why Ryan was finally there at that moment, she couldn't care though. She just needed her husband's arms around her after over a century.

His hand made its way to her shoulder and trailed down her arm to her hand, his warm fingers laced through her icy cold ones. She brought them to her lips and took in a deep breath.

"I would recognize that scent anywhere. I haven't smelled anyone quite like it in over a hundred years." She closed her eyes as she brought his hand to her chest.

He sat down behind her, his legs stretched out on either side. He wrapped his other arm around her waist and pulled her back into him. He rested his head on her shoulder, his lips dangerously close to her ear.

"I knew you remembered."

She shuddered at the feeling his hot breath made across her skin that flowed down to her core. She could instantly feel her temperature rising as she felt his soft kiss on the hollow just below her ear.

"Turn around, please."

"I can't."

"Why?"

"I'm so afraid it's all a dream. I've wished for this moment for so long, I just can't believe it's real."

He brought the back of his hand to caress her cheek. "Does this feel real?"

She dipped her cheek into his palm as her eyes softly shut. "Yes."

"Can you feel my lips here?" He placed another kiss at the base of her neck then pulled her clothes away from her skin, trailing kisses across her collarbone.

"Yes," she moaned.

"I'm real. I'm here. I'm not sure for how long, but I can't wait a minute longer."

He scooted back slightly as she slowly turned to face him, raising her slender fingers to his slightly stubbly cheek. She ran her thumb across the creases next to his eye as a tear escaped. She could hear his heart beating wildly in his chest, his pulse thumping through his veins.

"Not exactly how I left you, am I?"

She smiled at his words. "I think it was I that did the leaving, not that I ever intended to."

"I know. I know," he whispered, as he kissed her forehead. "Peter explained everything."

"Of course he did."

"I don't know how long I have."

She put her finger to his lips. "I don't want to think about that now. I just need this." She brought her lips to his. Slowly caressing each others in unison, his tongue aching for entrance. She swallowed back the venom that was pooling at the back of her throat and let his tongue pass her lips. Their kiss became more passionate as she pulled him to her. Her fingers a mess through his silky, onyx strands, his hand pressing the small of her back into him.

He brought himself back, hoping for just a second, but her hands pressed back at his shoulders. "I need to take you home with me."

"Not a problem." He pressed another soft kiss to her lips. His arms surrounded her, holding on tight. In a small flash of light, they disappeared.

The pair of eyes that had been watching each second from the tree line closed. He took a deep breath and let the cold air wash over him. He felt the ache throughout his body. He knew he needed her and he would find a way to bring her back to him.

## Chapter Twelve

## Sleeping Dogs

Ian had been sleeping on the couch in the jet's cabin for about an hour. Sam seemed to think it was a safe time to talk to Becca about what the hell was going on.

He walked from the galley to sit in the empty seat across from her.

"He looks comfortable."

Becca looked up from the book she was reading to admire a sleeping Ian, again.

"Yep."

"What do I need to know about the two of you?" Sam raised an eyebrow as Becca tried to innocently look into his eyes. Sam wasn't buying it.

"It's nothing; he was just helping me with Abe. It just... wasn't something I was ready to face alone."

"Abe tried to explain what happened. Why didn't you tell me?"

She closed her book and tossed it aside with a sigh. "The Bureau wanted to keep it quiet. With all the otherworldly indications, they were afraid for public safety."

"You must know, he feels horrible."

"I'm sure he does, but it doesn't matter anymore. No matter how hard I try to imagine the way I loved Abe, I can't stop seeing him burn and beat me. I can't forget him raping me." She let a tear escape, but brushed it away quickly.

"So, you just throw yourself into an impossible situation?" Sam looked over to Ian.

"I'm helping Lily. She loves him and he obviously loves her. I want her to be happy for once."

"You know how much I care for both you and Lily, but it hurts me to see you doing this."

"Doing what?" She knew what he was getting at, but didn't want to admit it to herself.

"Falling for a man that is more than a little off limits. Is that how you're going to keep yourself safe? Loving a man you know you can never have?"

She shook her head, suddenly feeling a little disgusted with herself. "I can't help it. You think I want to feel this way? Do you know how badly I wish I could just forget those last weeks with Abe? We would've been married and had little part human babies by now!"

"Nephilim."

"What?"

"A child born of a human and an angel is called a Nephilim."

"Well, we'd have Nephilim babies then. Playing in a huge yard, going for long walks along the lake shore, teaching them how to ride bikes... being able to be in Abe's arms without that fear."

"You can be." Sam took Becca's hand from her lap and brought it to his lips. "If I have to, I can find a way to make those memories disappear."

"No, you can't do that. We have to catch him first. Gideon is still out there. He got to Abe which anyone else would have thought impossible." Her hand was shaking in his. She would want nothing more than to be rid of those memories, but until Gideon was erased from the universe, those memories would have to stay right where they were.

"Alright, I'll let it go for now. But when we get back, I'm kicking the search for Gideon into gear. I won't rest until he's paid for what he's done; to both of you." Sam let Becca's hands go as he cleared his throat.

Becca noticed Sam shift uncomfortably in his seat. She could tell he was nervous, and Sam was *never* nervous.

"And...?" She knew there was more and even with the most painful memories of her life brimming on the surface, she needed to know.

"How much do you really know about Gideon?" Sam questioned as he sat forward, his elbows resting on his knees as his hands clasped together.

"I know he's a demon with the power of foresight and possession. I know he gets off on suffering. What else is there to know?"

Sam wiped his hand across his jaw before bringing his direct attention to Becca and what he had to tell her.

"Gideon has been around for eons, or so I'm told. It wasn't until someone very close to me died that we truly knew the effects his possession had on the human body." Becca raised her eyebrows in question. "Prolonged possession causes permanent changes in the brain, tumors mostly."

His words hit her chest like a wild tornado. Her insides began to shred and shudder as she braved to ask. "My mother?"

"Yes." Sam grabbed Becca's shaking hands and held them in his own once again. "He was very good at what he did. No one had a clue until it was too late. Your mother came to my office one morning pretty much hysterical. She had gotten you off to school and started into work when she heard the date on the radio – she lost three months. She had no memory of anything that happened during that time. I immediately got her to our physicians and they did a full body MRI, but the tumor they found was far too advanced. I called in fellow healers and shamans from the ends of the earth, but there wasn't anything to be done. That's when she made Lily and I promise to watch out for you, to protect you from Gideon. We both failed."

Sam's head fell, his chin hitting his chest.

"He's very powerful, and I know that when he really wants something, he's going to get it. What scares me the most is that now I know he is far from done with me." Becca replied, wiping a traitorous tear from her cheek.

"I've spent so many years researching, and I finally know how to kill him. Now I just have to find him."

"You know how?" Becca sniffled, while meeting her eyes with his.

Sam's attention was drawn away from Becca as Ian started to wake.

"Please tell me I've been asleep for ten hours and we're almost there," Ian yawned, as he stretched his arms above his head.

"Sorry, sleepy head. I think we're still somewhere over the Atlantic." Becca quickly brought her hand to wipe across her face making sure she'd gotten rid of every tear.

Ian got up and decided to take the seat next to Becca. "Do we have any sort of plan once we get there?"

"I've narrowed it down to a little town not far from Reykjavik." Becca pulled out a file from her bag as Sam smiled. "I have a feeling we are on the right track" she said, taking Sam's smile for confirmation as she pulled out the photo of the cottage she knew Lily was making her home.

# Chapter Thirteen

# Into The Mystic

Lily and Ryan fell onto her black leather couch after their whirlwind travel through space.

"Whoa! Is it always like that?"

Ryan's lips formed a curvaceous smile. "Yeah, but I've gotten used to it."

"There's so much I don't know. So much I want to ask, but I'm not sure I want to go back there." Lily cast her gaze into her lap at her entwined fingers.

Ryan tilted her chin to look into her eyes before cupping her cheek. "I'll tell you anything you want to know. One thing you need to understand is that whatever was done while we were forced apart has no bearing on what we are to each other. I promised to love you forever, and over a hundred years later, I am here telling you I love you more than I ever thought was possible. I don't care that I'm an angel and you're a vampire. For whatever time we have together, I just want to love you."

Lily's cheek was amazingly pink by the time Ryan removed his hand. She raised her hand to her warm cheek. "I didn't even realize I was doing it. I'm sorry. Are you alright?"

"What do you mean?" Ryan brushed a strand of her hair behind her ear with slight confusion.

"When you put your hand on my cheek, I absorbed your heat. Sometimes it makes people woozy if I do it for too long."

"You can take away other's body heat?"

"Yeah, it's my special 'super power', as Mr. Fleming calls it." She let out a soft laugh before he took both of her hands in his.

"How does it work, exactly?"

"It's pretty simple; if I touch someone I can absorb some of their body heat. When I concentrate, I can control how little or how much I absorb. It can be dangerous if I take too much. I've never killed a human, but have come close. I hope I never have to."

Ryan took her in his arms, bringing her to rest against his chest. "I really don't think you can hurt me, no matter how much heat you take." He laid a soft kiss in her hair as she took his hand and began tracing small circles on it.

"So, you want to tell me what you've been up to for the last hundred years?"

He let out a soft laugh at her directness. "Well..." He took a deep breath in preparation of launching into his story. "I searched for you for well over a year with the authorities. After they'd given up, I searched on my own. After eight years, my mother sat me down and told me in no uncertain terms that I had to let you go. I never remarried or even thought of doing so. I did become a father though."

Lily turned in Ryan's arms to face him. "You what?"

"It's not what you think." He caressed her cheek before threading his fingers though the soft tendrils at her temple. "My sister, Beatrice, married about a year after we did, but her husband, Harold, was killed in the war about five years later. They had a little boy named Denning. My sister became ill suddenly and died when the boy was just nine. Just before she died, she asked me to care for the boy. You know how close Bea and I were, so I took him in and devoted what I could of my life to becoming a good father and role model."

"I'm so happy you were able to be there for him. I thought of us with children so many times over the years. I wished that you could have been there when I took Becca in."

"The little girl in the locket?"

Lily smiled thinking of her first mother's day gift. "Yes, her mother, Anne, died of a brain tumor when Becca was only eight. We were all very close and even though I had no idea what I was doing, I took Becca in and raised her as best as I could. Funny thing is, she's actually an FBI agent, if you can believe it."

"She's still alive then?"

"Oh, yes. She just turned thirty-one this past summer. I miss her like crazy, but I had to get away."

"Yes." Ryan cleared his throat before taking Lily's hands in his own. "I read part of your journal. Ian seems like a very special man..."

Lily's chest immediately began to ache at the thought of Ryan knowing the intimacy she'd shared with Ian. "He was very special, but he's not you. Now that I have you back, I don't think I can ever let you go."

"Peter said he would try to keep everyone off my back for as long as he could, but I'll have to go back to my job, I guess you'd call it, eventually." He brought his lips down to hers for a soft kiss.

"How does it work? What do you do when you're not helping souls cross over?" Lily looked into his eyes with great curiosity.

"I can usually do anything I want. I often spend a great bit of time watching after Denning's six grandchildren. They are scattered around the globe so I get a chance to see quite a bit of the world. I love going to Rome though. I feel so much peace there with all the beauty and architecture."

Lily's eyes lit up at her memories of Rome. "Becca and I spent a lot of time there. I love the fountains at night; the water in the moonlight is breath-taking."

"We can go – right now if you like. We could be checked into a hotel in an hour and walking the streets by tonight. We can finish the honeymoon we never had a chance to." Ryan's eyes pleaded with hers.

"I think I'd like that. If I remember correctly, there are a few things we still had yet to try. Though, I'm not sure Peter or the man upstairs would approve." Lily smirked as a spark of recognition passed over Ryan's face.

"You are still my wife and how we choose to spend our honeymoon is none of their concern."

"My thoughts exactly." Lily's arms surrounded Ryan's neck pulling his lips to hers, engaging in the first of many kisses to begin their honeymoon over a hundred years late.

🥀 🌱 🥀

"Dare il Benvenuto all'Hotel de Russie." The female desk clerk greeted Ryan and Lily as they approached the front desk at the Hotel de Russie in Rome.

"Lei parla gli ingles?" Ryan asked, questioning if the woman spoke English in his perfect Italian accent.

"Yes, sir. How can we assist you this evening?"

Ryan smiled as he squeezed Lily's fingers as they clasped around his own.

"We are checking in. The reservation is under Ryan Edwards."

The clerk entered his name into her computer to bring up the reservation that suddenly appeared in the hotel's database. "Yes, here we have it. We have you in the Picasso Suite."

"Ryan," Lily sighed. "It's perfect." She brought him down to meet her lips.

"I just need to see both of your identifications and credit card." The clerk's smile was directed at Ryan as he pulled the needed items from his jacket pocket.

Lily looked at him a little confused as he produced two perfect replicas of British passports and a Master Card with Ryan's name embossed on it.

Ryan leaned down to whisper in her ear. "Just another one of the perks of working for the Big Guy."

Lily attempted to control the feeling of giddiness welling up inside her as the clerk finished checking them in. Ryan stroked the back of her left hand, noticing that there was most certainly something missing.

"Georgio will show you to your suite. Do you need a cart for your luggage?" The clerk looked them both over noticing that Lily was only carrying a black leather satchel, no luggage was to be seen.

"Unfortunately, our luggage was lost in transit." Lily explained sweetly while turning to look for Ryan to finish her thought.

"We will just be buying some new things in the meantime. What a way to celebrate our second honeymoon, my sweet?"

The clerk eyed them as Lily stood on her toes to place a soft kiss on Ryan's lips. "Second honeymoon? How long have you been married, if I may ask?"

Both Ryan and Lily let out a soft laugh before Lily could answer. "I remember it as if it was yesterday, but it has actually been some time."

"And now that we are here, we have some celebrating to do." Ryan looked to the clerk for their suite card key.

"Yes, Mr. Edwards." She handed over the card to Ryan. "Don't hesitate to call for any of your needs. Have a wonderful stay."

"We will," Lily uttered, before dragging her husband to the elevator to their suite.

"Posso mostrarla alla sua suite." Georgio stated, explaining that he could show them up to their suite.

"Nessun bisogno. Possiamo trovare la postra maniera." Ryan replied, letting the young Georgio know they could find their own way.

ଞ ඟ ଛ

Their suite was bathed in the glowing moonlight pouring in from the balcony doors. They wandered through the suite's lounge hand in hand until they reached the bedroom.

"That's a big bed." Lily shuddered as she took in the magnitude of the moment. She could feel the heat radiating from Ryan's skin warming her own.

"That it is. Nothing like that little paper thin mattress on the train." His hand moved from within hers to the small of her back.

"Not even close."

Ryan kissed Lily's cheek before pulling back to show her his mischievous grin. Before she knew it, Ryan had run full force, jumping into the middle of the bed. He rolled from his stomach to his back, getting comfortable amongst the fluffy bedding.

The shock on Lily's face was evident. She'd remembered how playful human Ryan was in their younger days, but wasn't sure how much angel Ryan would let loose.

He patted the bed next to him while raising his eyebrows up and down. "It's very comfortable, maybe even more than the one at the cottage. Care to join me?"

Lily dropped her satchel at the foot of the bed before crawling up next to Ryan on all fours. She lay on her side, her head finding the perfect spot in the crook of his neck. Ryan's arms wrapped around Lily's waist as her fingers walked their way up the buttons of his black dress shirt.

"I don't know what Peter told you, but it took me quite a while to remember anything but my name from my human life." She took the top button of his shirt and removed it from its hole.

"You know how vague Peter can be," Ryan replied, as he began stroking lightly at the small of her back where a sliver of skin was exposed. "He really didn't tell me much."

"After the train, a vampire named Martin found me – saved me actually." She helped another button release from his shirt. "I could feel myself dying. It was as if my body and soul were separating. Then it all went quiet, like I was floating in a wisp of serenity and peace. When I came to, Martin asked my name. I told him it was Lily. He began asking me all sorts of questions and my mind kept flipping through all these images of you, but I couldn't remember who you were." She let her fingers slip beneath his shirt to caress the downy hair on his chest. Her fingertip slowly made patterns across his heart which she felt beating rapidly. "You'd come to me in all my dreams, but you never told me your name."

"How..." He took in another breath as she pulled at one side of his shirt and three buttons released all at once. "How did you finally remember?"

She pulled his shirt apart, letting it rest at his sides, before crawling further on top of him to place a gentle kiss over his heart. She then rested her chin on his sternum and looked up into his eyes. "Martin was essentially a father figure, and as a father he wanted his daughter happily coupled off with a mate. He introduced me to Jean Paul, a vampire who had been turned during the French Revolution when he was just twenty-three. Martin thought we could be perfect for each other, but every time I thought of even coming close to him I saw your face." Her fingertips lazily traced the defined contours of his jaw. "I remembered your eyes and the way they lit up every time you saw me. I remembered how soft your lips were every time we kissed." Her fingertips softly tread across his lips. "Jean Paul was a very passionate young man, very adventurous. He got swept up in a moment one night we were out and pulled me into a passionate kiss."

Ryan rolled his eyes as he squirmed underneath her.

She smacked his chest lightly. "Stop. He was a wonderful man, but when he kissed me everything came flooding back. Growing up in Boston, my parents, moving to London... The first time we snuck off to the kitchen and you kissed me right after we had finished off one of Emily's apple pies... It was all there."

"So, what happened with Jean Paul?" He raised his eyebrows as he stroked his fingers through her hair starting at her temple.

"We had fun together, but nothing romantic ever happened after that. Even being the second man I'd ever kissed, he was nothing compared to you."

"And Ian? How did he compare?"

Her head dipped down, her lips flush with the skin of his chest. "He reminded me so much of you," she mumbled into his chest.

"A ruggedly handsome bloke, then?"

She looked up with a smile. "Yes, very handsome, but his mannerisms too. His playfulness and his eyes. He gave me a flutter and I tried to see where it would take me, but I let it get too serious; hence my move to Iceland."

"Do you feel a flutter now?" He leaned down, his lips meeting her forehead.

"More like a raging inferno. No one else ever came close to making me feel what I am at this moment."

"Inferno? Hmm... Let's see if we can warm you up a bit more." He sat them both up then tore his shirt from his shoulders. "It might be a tad bit unconventional, but I think every stitch of clothing needs to go." He grasped them hem of her navy cotton t-shirt and swiftly pulled it over her head.

She reached in between her breasts to unclasp her burgundy bra, before sliding it off her shoulders and down her torso. She seized his shoulders, pulling his chest flush with hers and in a breath, their lips met. The heat from his breath entered her mouth with every kiss, flowing deeper and deeper inside of her until she felt she might melt at any second.

His hands went to the front of her jeans, pulling at the button then the zipper. He nibbled on her bottom lip as he spoke. "This was a lot easier when it was just a dressing gown. I think I hate zippers."

"Me too." She pulled on his with a little too much force, ripping one side of his jeans from seam to seam across his thigh.

They instantly pulled back from each other, inspecting for any real damage.

"Oops." Lily batted her eyelashes innocently before Ryan grabbed her arms and flipped her onto her back.

He sat on his haunches between her legs, removing each shoe and then pulling her legs out of her jeans one leg at a time. He was rewarded with the sight of a pair of matching burgundy lace boy shorts. He licked his lips before jumping off the bed and ridding himself of his shoes and ripped jeans.

She turned and sat on the edge of the bed bringing his upright form closer. She began to lay long soft kisses around his navel as he massaged her scalp.

"Things have really changed since the last time we were together." Lily's tongue traced a circle around Ryan's navel, her fingertips following the trail of hair leading down lower. "Some of the things I always wanted to try back then were so forbidden. Now, I..."

Ryan slipped his fingers under her chin bringing her gaze to his. "I want to touch, kiss, and taste every inch of your body. I know if we would have had more time we would have explored each other fully. I want to give you the pleasure I never had a chance to, just tell me what you want. I'm yours."

She smiled against his stomach as she wrapped her arms around his waist. Her fingers slipped into the back of his black boxer briefs making their way to the front before tugging them down. He kicked them off and looked down to see her admiring his hardened length. She looked up at him, silently asking for permission. A soft nod and a caress of her cheek gave her the courage to continue. Her fingers flowed lightly over the silky soft skin, the veins began pulsating beneath her palm as she slowly began to stroke.

"Lily, that feels..." Ryan groaned before struggling for air taking short gasping breaths.

She leaned in with closed eyes and reverently kissed the tip. Once, twice, three times before she braved to open her mouth a little wider. She was stopped by Ryan scooping her up beneath her arms and throwing her into the middle of the bed.

He hovered above her, his fingers teasing at her lace. "May I?"

All she could do was nod, any other thought escaping her.

He pulled the lace from her hips and down her legs, throwing it off to the side to join the rest of their forgotten clothing.

He layered kisses from one hip to the other with light sweeps of his tongue in between. His hands lightly massaged her thigh, opening her up to him. His breath swept over her stomach, reaching her breast as he began to suckle on her nipple. Her breath hitched at the powerful sensations surging throughout her body. The long, languid licks that at one time would have made her blush ten shades of red were common place at that moment. She whimpered at the feeling of his thumb lightly tracing one nipple while he kissed, tugged, and bit at the other.

Her moans reverberated off the bedroom walls causing both of them to continue to ache where they needed each other most. Her fingers tangled through his onyx strands while his lips traveled across her collarbone and up her neck. She felt him teasing at her entrance as his lips hovered above hers.

"Ryan." She brought her hand from his hair to caress his cheek, attempting to keep her body from writhing off the bed. "Don't make me wait any longer."

"I aim to please, my sweet." His lips met hers as she felt him slowly slide into her.

She groaned as he slid in and out of her. Her muscles began to pulsate around him as his thrusts became deeper and longer. The sweat dripped from his brow as they each came closer to the release they'd waited over a century for. Her fingertips dug at his hips as she pulled him in. His breath fanned across her breast which seemed to be directly linked to her undulating core.

He sped up with her encouragement, thrusting without thought or rhythm. His breaths were coming in short pants as he couldn't hold himself back anymore.

"Are you with me?" he whispered.

"Yes!" Her muscles convulsed around him and she felt him empty himself into her.

The panting slowed down as he lay spent with his head on her chest. He kissed the side of her left breast, his breath flowing across her nipple.

"That was worth the wait."

She sighed and brought her lips down to the crown of his head. "Definitely."

"You know the best part about us being the way we are now?" He questioned, as he slipped from within her and lay on his side next to her.

She raked her hand through her hair, attempting to control the mess they had created. "No. I can't see the upside in us being apart for this long and me being a blood-sucking vampire while you ferry souls to the other side for the man upstairs." She turned to look into his eyes and was met with his brow scrunched up in an irritated glare.

"What I mean is that we have an unending supply of stamina for all the make-up sex, which I hear is the best kind." He leaned in and placed as soft peck on her nose.

"Make-up sex? I thought that was for only after a fight, or so I've been told." Her fingers made their way to his temple to sweep the sweat drenched hair from his forehead.

"Ah, but this is 'make-up for lost time' sex. I know how much we talked about making love before we were married and we only got to put it into practice a few times, but-"

"Eight times," she interrupted. "Eight perfect times."

"Yes, eight, you're right – but we have a century to make up for. Peter himself is going to have to drag me away. I don't ever want to be away from you again. I've never stopped loving you, not for one second of eternity."

She placed her forehead against his. "Nor I you. I tried so hard to forget, but even this un-beating heart of mine would never let go of you. He must have a plan for us. Maybe this was how we were supposed to be all along."

"I have no idea." He brought his lips to hers, brushing delicately across them. "Whatever His plan is, I hope we figure it out soon."

They heard a knocking on their suite door at that moment. They looked at each other, then to their bedroom door. "Speak of He and He shall arrive. Or maybe it's just Peter here to spoil all our fun."

Lily got out of bed and pulled on a hotel issued robe, making her way out of the bedroom to the front door of their suite to find the person behind the disruption of their reunion.

## Chapter Fourteen

## Fight And Flight

So many things flew through Becca's mind for the remainder of the flight. Finding out that Gideon was the reason behind her mother's death made her comb through all the memories she had of her mother in the last year of her life.

She tried so hard to remember, but it had been at least twenty-two years. Twenty-two years of trying to forget. Little things popped out here and there, but nothing overly odd. She did remember lots of weekend trips to The Manchester Group offices. Becca remembered getting her own security card so that she was able to explore the building on her own while her mother worked on... She really couldn't remember what her mother had been working on.

Sam had made special arrangements for them to land at Reykjavik Airport. Normally, private international flights didn't land there, but when you had the money of The Manchester Group in the palm of your hand, almost anything was possible.

Once they had gathered their bags, they made their way to the car park. A black sedan was waiting with a driver holding a sign that read 'Fleming'.

Sam approached the driver and shook his hand. "I'm Sam Fleming. These are my companions, Ian Holt and Rebecca Swift."

The young man shook each of their hands before introducing himself. "Liam Caldwell. I've been instructed to be at your disposal. You have reservations in town, but I was told we would be going somewhere else first."

Becca could barely see Liam's eyebrows rise behind his dark aviator glasses. She looked to Sam to answer the man as they loaded the bags into the trunk.

"We were hoping to spend the day in Seltjarnarnes. We are looking to surprise a friend that lives close." Sam tightened his wool coat around him as Liam shut the trunk lid.

"Beautiful part of the country up there. I'm sure your friend will be happy to see you." Liam opened the back passenger side door. "Miss Swift?" He motioned for Becca to enter the back of the car.

She slid in, slightly relaxing as her backside took comfort in the heated leather seat. Ian slid in next to her shivering while Sam sat up front with Liam.

"When you said cold weather, you really meant it." Ian cupped his hands in front of his mouth and tried to blow his hot breath on them.

"This is nothing. Hopefully we won't have a blizzard while we're here." Becca replied, resting her head on the back of the seat as the car began to move.

"Oh, come on. No snowmen or snow angels for you?"

She turned her head and gave him her best glare, but it soon melted once she noticed the pouting lip and bright blue eyes pleading with her.

She straightened up in her seat and looked out the front window before she spoke again. "Once we find Lily, I have a feeling we won't be spending time together goofing off in the snow." She could feel the very real ache in her chest grow as she spoke the words she knew to be true. She was doing her best to keep herself together when she felt Ian's cool hand grasp her own.

"No matter what happens from here on out, you will always be a huge part of my life. You've given me something I thought I'd never have again; Hope."

Becca swallowed hard before turning her gaze back to him. "I'm glad I could help. Lily deserves all the happiness in the world."

"You do too." She felt a soft squeeze of her hand which sent a sharp pain straight to her heart. "You'll find it. Someone as amazing as you are deserves to be shared. Any guy would be lucky to have someone as beautiful, funny, and smart as you."

"Thanks." Becca let out a deep breath before taking her hand out of Ian's. She faked a yawn and laid her head back against the seat. "I hardly slept a wink on the plane. I think it's catching up with me."

"Rest. I'll wake you once we get there."

Becca smiled and fluttered her eyes closed. She concentrated on Ian's breathing as she slowly relaxed and actually fell asleep.

Ian's gaze stayed on Becca as her breathing evened out and his mind began to wander. He began to think about the words he'd just spoken to her.

*"Someone as amazing as you deserves to be shared."*

The ache in his chest was a familiar one, but not where Becca was concerned. He'd felt the ache in a thousand different degrees since Lily had left him, but when Becca showed up it was replaced by the feeling of hope she'd brought with her. He wondered why Becca finding someone to spend her life with would cause the feeling to return.

He thought about the way they had ended up talking like old friends the night she arrived in Boston. They talked about anything and everything, and had discovered they had so much in common outside of Lily. They loved to cook, enjoyed the same type of music, and even liked to dance on occasion.

The sudden vision of he and Becca dancing at one of his father's many political functions came to mind. He could see the blue silk perfectly formed around her curves, almost feel it beneath his fingertips as they caressed her backside. The thought brought a smile to his lips, yet he wondered why he had never thought of Lily in that way.

He was brought out his vivid thoughts as the car pulled up outside a tavern and came to a stop. Sam stepped out after instructing Liam to wait for them all in the car.

Becca slowly woke as Sam opened her door and took her hand.

"We're here," Sam whispered.

Becca straightened up before sliding out to stand on the street. Ian came around the back of the car to join Becca and Sam.

"You ready for this?" Sam looked to Ian but was really addressing them both.

"As I'll ever be," Ian answered, as he placed his hand on the small of Becca's back.

They walked up to the front door and entered the charming local tavern.

They noticed a petite redheaded woman wiping down the bar once they were all inside. The rest of the tavern was empty.

"Sorry 'bout the mess. We haven't really been open for regular business for a couple of days." The woman busied herself with cleaning a few glasses as the three of them approached the bar. "What can I..."

The woman's gaze froze on Becca. "I can't believe it. You're Rebecca!" The woman rushed around the bar to give Becca bone-crushing a hug.

"Yes, and you are?"

Renee pulled herself back with a flush of embarrassment across her cheeks. "Oh, right. I'm sure Lily hadn't mentioned me, but I thought maybe Peter would have. I thought I made a pretty good impression. Anyway, I'm Renee. This is my place."

"Wait, slow down." Sam stood in front of Renee. "You know Lily and Peter?"

"Well, I've known Lily since she bought the cabin a few years back. Peter came just a few days ago. I thought maybe bringing her sister here was the surprise he had promised."

Sam shook his head while his eyes were squeezed shut. He lifted his head to see Renee's excited eyes.

"I'm sorry, I've been rude. I'm Sam Fleming. Lily used to work for me." He then motioned to Becca. "This is Rebecca Swift, as you know, Lily's sister." Sam stepped next to Ian and clasped his hand on his shoulder. "This is Ian Holt."

Ian stepped forward to shake Renee's hand. "Has Lily mentioned me?"

"I'm sorry, no. Are you another brother of hers? You don't really look like Peter, though." Renee looked slightly confused as Sam brought her attention back to him.

"No, no. Ian is a close friend of the family." He placed his hand gently on Renee's shoulder. "When was the last time you spoke with Lily?"

"Sometime yesterday. She left here after we talked about the surprise Peter would be leaving for her. I take it by all of your faces, your visit is not the surprise."

"Peter didn't send us, no. Lily doesn't know we're coming. Do you think you might give her a call and see if she could come here? We'd appreciate it." Sam's fingertips made their way down to Renee's hand.

"Sure." Renee went back behind the bar and grabbed the phone.

Sam noticed Becca being calmed by Ian from what looked like a minor panic attack. Sam went over to them and tried to explain the situation.

"What was Peter doing here?" Becca was noticeably frazzled. "We haven't seen him since the whole Gideon mess. Doesn't he only come around when, He," she pointed upwards, "has something for her to do?"

"Yes, but I hadn't heard anything that would need her specific attention. Nothing Debir or Filipp couldn't handle."

Ian's breath had regulated as he looked to Sam confused. "Who are they?"

"The only other vampires in known existence. They work for us, thankfully." Sam sighed as he thought about the two of them working together in Bucharest.

"She's the only female vampire?" Ian shout whispered.

"Calm down." Sam ushered the three of them to a nearby table to sit down. "Yes. That is why she knows how important it is that we know where she is at all times; she had to tell me where she would be."

"I hope a few draughts are alright." Renee placed three glasses of amber liquid on their table. "Lily's not answering at home or on her cell. I called work, but she's not there either."

"Is that unusual?" Becca asked before taking a sip. "Wow, this is really good."

"Thanks. But yeah, it is a little. She never turns her cell off." Renee stood with her hands on her hips deep in thought.

At that moment, the front door opened and closed. Liam stood at the door. His hand reached back to the door and turned the lock before switching the sign to 'closed'.

Sam stood to address Liam. "I thought I'd asked you to stay in the car."

"Plans have changed, Sammael."

Sam swallowed hard, as shock of his true name being spoken surged through him. He felt Becca stand next to him and take his hand.

"Oh, and the beautiful Rebecca. I've been waiting a long time for this moment. I'll have to adjust my plans a little to accommodate Mr. Holt, but no bother. More incentive for our favorite immortal."

Rebecca shuddered at Sam's side as Ian slowly rose next to her, his hand grasping her hip tightly.

"I don't know who you think you are, but you're not welcome here," Renee stated, as she approached Liam and attempted to shoo him towards the door.

He pulled out what looked like a ballpoint pen before pressing the tip into Renee's bicep. Within a second, she fell unconscious to the floor.

"Now that she's out of the way, shall we be going?" Liam stepped over Renee's body while placing the pen back into his pocket.

"What have you done?" Becca's voice came out as a strangled cry.

"She'll wake up, I think." Liam smiled as he removed his aviator glasses to reveal the purest blue eyes.

"You can't be, your kind died out decades ago..." Sam took a protective stance in front of Becca and Ian.

"Tsk, tsk, tsk. You know better than to underestimate us." Liam rolled up his sleeve to reveal a small, black circle of flames embedded in the skin at his wrist. "Maybe The Manchester Group isn't as all knowing as you thought." Liam rubbed his hands together in excitement. "Shall we get this show on the road?"

"What do you think you're going to do? You can't have any real powers having never been really fed on." Sam was confident in his assessment as he stood tall in front of Becca and Ian.

"No, but I do have this."

Liam pulled out a small box from his jacket pocket. The top split open into four angled pieces. A red orb glowed increasingly brighter as he brought it up for Sam to examine.

"Bye-bye." The red glow encompassed the tavern completely before the four of them disappeared, leaving Renee unconscious on the floor.

ଣ ᴡ ଥ

Abe hadn't left for Iceland as early as he had wanted. He planned on arriving before Becca did, but he had appeared at the airport just seconds before she and her companions drove off in the black sedan.

He waited in an alley across from the tavern that they had entered and noticed the driver get out and go in a few moments later. He was prepared to wait a while, when he saw all the windows in the tavern glow with a bright red light.

He rushed in, taking the door off its hinges, to find a young woman lying on the floor. No Becca, no Sam, not even Ian... He knelt down at the woman's side, trying to revive her.

She groaned as Abe lifted her up into his lap.

"Can you tell me what happened?" Abe questioned, as he brushed the hair from her face.

"I... I... I'm not sure." She focused on Abe's eyes and smiled. "I like your eyes. So big."

Abe let out a soft chuckle as he helped her up to the chair sitting next to them.

"I'm Abe, by the way. I was supposed to meet Sam here. I saw their car outside, and then there was a strange light coming from the window. Sorry about your door," He apologized, giving her a lopsided grin

"It's okay; I'll get one of the boys to fix it. I'm Renee." She smiled back at him with a slight blush gracing her cheeks.

"Can you remember what happened when my friends came in?" Abe pulled out the chair next to Renee and sat beside her.

"The three of them came in. I recognized Rebecca from some pictures Lily had of the two of them. They all introduced themselves and said they were here to visit Lily. I tried to call her but I couldn't reach her. Then this guy with these really blue eyes came in. I wasn't sure what he was going to do, but he looked like one of those guys that are all talk. I've dealt with those idiots time and time again, so I tried to kick him out. Obviously, that didn't work out too well 'cause the next thing I know, I'm waking up on the floor with you staring at me. Not that it was a bad way to wake up, just a little unexpected." She took a breath after practically running out. "Sorry, I let the words get away from me sometimes."

"It's perfectly alright. Do you think you can take me to Lily's place? Maybe I can figure out where she's gone from there."

"Sure, just let me call Ivan to come and fix the door." Renee stood a little too quickly and began her descent back to the floor, but Abe was there to catch her first. "Thanks. Whatever that guy gave me was pretty powerful stuff."

Abe helped Renee right herself before clearing his throat. "Yeah, let's hope he's not doing anything to my friends or Lily."

Renee nodded before slowly making her way behind the bar.

Abe settled back down into his chair, his mind racing in a thousand different directions. He knew if he could pick up a trail he could find them, but there was no trace left of Sam, Becca, or Ian in the tavern. There was a hint of Lily that he assumed would be even stronger where she lived.

He thought of using a talent he hardly ever used because he had such little control over it. He could survey a room and see what had occurred within a time period. The drawback of the power was that if anyone was with him, they would see it also. He never had control over how long the images would flash in front of his eyes or how long they would last. Not wanting to scare Renee he decided to wait until they were ready to go to Lily's to explain.

Abe watched as a large man with a slight eye twitch repaired the front door. Renee stood talking with the man, handing him several tools then taking short glances at Abe. He noticed her blush which only made her that much more endearing to him. He also noticed the way her hair fell in waves past her shoulders to the middle of her back, the way her lips formed a tiny heart shape when she smiled, how her green eyes sparkled when she blushed...

He shook the thoughts from his head as he noticed Renee saying goodbye to the twitchy eyed repairman. She came over with her coat and gloves already on.

"We should probably take my truck. It's used to the roads. It shouldn't be too bad, but just in case."

"I need to tell you a few things first if I may. You might want to sit down for this." He pulled out a chair for her, which she slowly took.

He sat in the chair across from her. "First, I'll let you know that I've known Lily for about seventy-five years."

"Get out!" Renee slapped the table with both hands. "The guy with the sleeper pen said something about an immortal. Are you both immortals?"

"In a way, yes. I'm a type of angel, a shadow walker to be more specific." Renee sat back in her chair with her hands covering her mouth, her eyes wide as saucers. "As for Lily, she's actually a vampire. Not your killing humans kind – she only drinks from animals."

"Wow. That kinda makes sense though. She's so beautiful and she never seems to eat anything. Then the other day when I was trying to wake her up, she wasn't breathing. It scared the crap out of me."

"You're taking this a lot better than I expected." Abe let out a soft laugh as he shook his head.

"I grew up in Southern California. I learned very early in life that the strangest things in life were often very real." She raised her eyebrows as she grabbed one of the abandoned glasses of ale and took a large gulp.

"Near El Centro?"

"Yeah, why?"

Abe slapped his hand on the table and laughed at his memories of the small town. "There was a group of devil worshipers there back in the nineties. They actually caused a pretty big mess, released a lot of demons. It was a messy clean up. I'm sure some even got away."

"Shit, really?"

"Really, but back to the little matter of our friends being abducted."

"Right. Yes, sorry." She put down her glass and gave Abe her full attention.

"I can do a sweep of a room and visualize the activities that have happened. If you're here, you'll see them too. They can go at different speeds and I can't control how far back they will go. Do you think you can handle it?"

Renee got a serious look on her face as she nodded her head. "As long as I can sit here, I think I'll be okay."

"Alright. Here we go."

Abe stood up and brought forth the images of the room. It started with what looked like a memorial service. A picture of a stocky man with Renee's eyes had its place on the bar as people stood next to it telling stories. It raced by fairly quickly up until the moment the driver guy walked in. Renee's body fell swiftly to the floor before he got a glimpse of the man's wrist and the markings embedded in his skin. He saw Sam's face fill with fear as the box with the red orb appeared. The glow filled the room and then they all just disappeared. It sped up to the moment the man was fixing the door. What were originally short glances between Abe and Renee became slow motion frames. By the time the images came back to the present and stopped, Abe and Renee were both flushed and slightly exhausted.

"What was that box thing?" Renee panted while she reached for her glass of ale.

"You really don't want to know. We should get going, but we don't need your truck." Abe stood in front of Renee, offering his hand. "Just take my hand and visualize Lily's place."

"Okay." Renee took his hand as Abe pulled her in his arms.

"Hold on tight."

ଔ ୴ ଶ

"That was awesome!" Renee was panting heavily, her head down and hands grasping her knees.

"You'll get used to it after a few times." Abe shrugged, trying to let her know it was no big deal.

"Alright, we're here. Do your thing."

Abe looked around Lily's living room thoroughly before concentrating on what he needed to know.

He saw a man with jet black hair snooping around the house, before placing a note and what looked like a ring on Lily's stove. Lily swiftly appeared and looked frantic as she read the note and began searching the house herself. More of a lot of nothing showed until Lily and the man appeared together cuddling on her couch. Then they were up and excited. Abe concentrated as hard as he possibly could to slow the scene down a bit. He was able to read their lips and find out they were going to Rome and that the man's name was Ryan.

In another blink they were gone and Abe was brought back into the present.

"Do you have any idea who that man was?" Abe turned to find Renee curled up in the corner of the couch.

"Nope, but she looked really happy. Like 'in love' kind of happy." Renee sighed. "I knew she had to have a guy. A woman that beautiful can't be alone forever."

"You'd be surprised," Abe replied, rolling his eyes at the knowledge of Lily's severe lack of male companions over the years. "It looks like they were off to Rome. You up for another adventure?"

Renee looked over to see Abe's sparkling eyes and mouth watering smile. "Rome? Yeah, of course! But, what about passports and stuff? Even if we travel like that, won't we need them?"

"Just let me take care of it." Abe stood up and pulled Renee into his arms. "It will last a little longer this time since we're going further."

"Right. I won't let go." Renee smiled at Abe before burying her face in his chest and placing a death grip around his rib cage.

Moments later, Abe and Renee were standing outside of a hotel suite. Abe was holding Renee upright as she attempted to catch her breath.

"Where...are...we?" She panted.

" 'Hotel de Russie' in Rome. This must be their room." Abe responded, as he began knocking on the door.

He heard footsteps approaching before the door swung open to reveal Lily in only a fluffy white hotel robe.

"Abe? Renee? What are you doing here? Together?"

"It's a long story." Abe pushed passed her into the suite as Renee grabbed onto Lily, following him in.

# Chapter Fifteen

## Roman Holiday

*T*housands of scenarios soared through Lily's mind as she made her way into the living area of the suite with Renee clutched to her side. She could never of prepared herself for the meeting she was about to have with three very different individuals.

Abe plunked himself down on the couch facing the opened terrace doors. "Nice view."

"Uh...Thanks?" Lily didn't really know how to respond. She hadn't seen Abe since the day he and Becca escaped from Gideon, and she had never really expected to see him again.

"Did you order champagne or something?" Ryan entered the living area wearing a robe identical to Lily's. He surveyed the room and took in their guests. "Friends of yours?"

"Yes." She took Renee from her side and sat her down next to Abe, then motioned for Ryan to come stand beside her.

"I'm not sure how to..." Lily looked to Renee with a tilt of her head and brows furrowed.

"It's cool. Abe told me about the whole vampire thing. And that he's an angel or something." Renee sat nodding for Lily to go on.

"Okay." She turned to Ryan to begin her introductions. "Ryan, this is Abe North. He is a shadow walker and works for The Manchester Group. This little spit-fire is Renee. She's my friend from Seltjarnarnes, she owns the tavern there." Then she looked to the two that were sitting on the couch. "And to you two, this is Ryan Edwards. He's an agent of Peter's and...my husband."

Renee squealed and jumped up, bringing Lily into a tight hug while Abe sat there noticeably shocked.

"You got married in Rome? How romantic! Was it beautiful? I'm sure it was beautiful. I'm so happy for you!" Renee let it all out in a rush as she swayed Lily violently from side to side.

"No, we were already married." Lily answered as she peeled Renee off of her.

"Her human husband?" It was meant as a question, but Abe said it more like a statement of fact.

"Yes, we were married in 1905. Late spring, if I recall correctly." Ryan wrapped his arm around Lily's waist. "We've just now found out where we both ended up and were in the middle of a second honeymoon, but I guess you're here to cut that short." He raised his eyebrows to Abe.

"Yes. I'm sorry to say, Becca had tracked you to Seltjarnarnes. She had Sam and her fiancé with her."

"Fiancé?" Lily questioned. "I just spoke with her; she never mentioned anything to me."

"I don't know how recent it was but he made it pretty clear the other day in my office that she was his alone." Abe scrubbed his hands over his face in noticeable frustration.

"That Ian guy was her fiancé?" Renee bit down on her lip in clear confusion. "They didn't tell me that."

Lily had brought her hands to her head, shaking as she squeezed her eyes shut. "Ian Holt?"

"Oh, that's just not right." Ryan shook his head as Lily made her way over to the chair.

"That's what he said his name was. Is that why you think she came to find you? To tell you about the wedding?" Renee asked, as though it was the most logical conclusion.

"I don't know." She squinted as she looked to Abe for some sort of answer. "Where are they now then?"

"That's why we are here. Did you know the Ahbmonites had resurfaced?"

If Lily could have gone any paler at that moment, she would have. Flashes of the man with jet black hair and pure blue eyes flooded her mind. The small symbol on the inside of his wrist burning its way into the permanent recesses of her brain.

"I wasn't sure, but I guess you are telling me they have." Lily lolled her head to the side, cupping her jaw with her hand propped up on the arm of the chair.

"They called him Liam, if that helps," Renee spoke up cautiously, obviously realizing the severity of the situation.

"I never knew his name, but I felt it – the pull that Martin told me about. It scared the hell out of me, if I'm being honest. Once I realized what was happening, I got out of there as fast as I could." Ryan gently began massaging her shoulders in attempt to ease the tension of the conversation.

"Well, this guy is one of them, markings and all and he has Becca, Sam, and Ian."

Lily sat straight up in her chair. "What! How?!"

"An Anarcori. Remember that little gold box with the red orb that was lost in the twenties?" Lily nodded. "He's got it and he knows how to use it. I don't see how he can be alone on this one."

"Hold on just a moment." Ryan came around the side of Lily's chair to face her. "What exactly is an Ahbmonite and why would he take your friends?"

Lily looked to Abe for any sort of explanation, but he had none. She then rose from her chair and pushed Ryan down into it.

"There are so many legends about how vampires came into existence; some even saying that Judas Iscariot was one of the first, after his transgressions with Jesus of Nazareth. From all that I learned from my sire, Martin, the line we come from started long ago in Jerusalem." Lily took a deep unnecessary breath before moving on.

"According to Martin and all the books that we have held over the years, the Ahbmonites were basically food for a quartet of vampires. The four, all males, found the odd race of humans fascinating. They were drawn to them unlike any other human, not to kill them but for them to nurture each other. The vampires fed from a type of blood they never had tasted before and the Ahbmonites acquired vampire traits strengthened in them with each feeding. When their human bodies could no longer handle the vampire traits, they were either killed or turned. After a few centuries, the families began branding their children with the mark of the black flame. Martin's sire was one of the Ahbmonites, but he believed that it was time for their race to end. Stop using humans as cattle and learn to live off the blood of animals. That fight eventually led to the practical extinction of the vampire race. Now, only three of us remain."

Ryan held out his hand in invitation. She took it and snuggled into his lap as visions of blue eyes and black flames raced through her mind.

"He took them to use as leverage against you?" Abe looked up at Lily as her gaze met his.

"I'm not sure of any other explanation. If this Liam is the same man I encountered in Las Vegas, he knew all about me and wanted to be my companion." She felt Ryan's hand moving up and down her spine attempting to soothe the strained muscles.

"So, you drank from this guy and now he's got some vampire traits, enough that he could take all three of them?" Renee inquired.

Lily turned to Ryan and nodded shamefully. "I'd never felt that kind of pull ever in my existence as a vampire. It was truly some sort of biological connection, like somehow we were made for each other. As though our existence depended on one another."

"What now? We just sit around and wait for him to call?" Renee was full of questions, yet all completely relevant.

"I'd need to get to Martin's library. All of his books are stored there. It's just outside of Reading."

Renee straightened up in her seat. "You mean the Reading that's in the UK? I've never been to the UK."

"Looks like today's your lucky day." Abe took Renee's hand, lacing his fingers through hers before patting her hand.

Lily noticed Abe's movements wondering exactly what the meanings behind them were.

Renee's face tinged a slight shade of pink and her heart rate increased as each pass of Abe's thumb caressed the heel of her hand. Lily had seen that look on Renee's face before, the day she met Peter. It was attraction; and from the looks of it, the feeling was mutual.

Lily shook herself out of the haze created by Abe and Renee to focus on the task at hand. "I'll just make a call to Jefferson. He is the caretaker for several houses in the area. I'll need to let him know we will be coming to stay for a few days." Lily lifted herself from Ryan's lap to retrieve her cell phone from the bedroom. She stopped as she reached the door, turning back to the rest of them. "We just need to get dressed and gather a few things. We should be ready to go in a few minutes. You remember where it is, Abe?"

Abe swallowed hard as images of his trip with Lily and Becca began to surface. "Yes, I think I can recall the way."

Lily entered the bedroom and retrieved her phone from the dresser. She dialed Jefferson's number and heard his voice only after two rings.

"Ah, old girl. It's been a while."

She let out a soft laugh at the voice of her old friend. "Jefferson, how many times have I told you to call me Lily?"

"Every time we talk, but that's neither here nor there. What can I do for you?"

"I'm going to be using the house for a couple of days – well, myself and three friends to be more accurate. Will that be a problem?"

"Not if you don't mind getting wet. It's been pouring on and off for days and has shown no sign of stopping."

"We'll be fine. Actually, we will be arriving in about an hour or so."

"It'll be good to see you again. I hope you'll be staying for a while, the house was meant to be used for more than just a holiday."

Lily ran her fingers through her dark tresses as she bit down on her lip. "I know. I hope I can spend more time there now. We'll see what happens."

"Alright, little miss. I'll drop in and check on you tomorrow."

"I'll see you then. Thank you, Jefferson."

"Not a problem. Tomorrow."

"Tomorrow." She ended the call to notice Ryan standing just inside the bedroom with the door closed behind him.

"I'm sure we'll find what we need, my sweet."

Lily walked over to him, her arms slipping around his waist as her cheek pressed against his chest. "I don't know what I would do without her."

He kissed the top of her head while his eyes squeezed tightly shut. "I'll make sure you won't have to."

The sudden realization of the situation flipped a switch inside her. Her anger came bubbling to the surface ready to devour all in its path. "I just can't believe all of this! This Liam guy took three of the most important people in my life; how am I supposed to think it's not about me?" She gasped, as all her thoughts came rushing out. She pulled away from Ryan and began to pace in front of him.

"And what is all of that about Becca being engaged to Ian? How the hell did *that* happen? I mean, what the shit is that?!" She glanced to see Ryan giving her a subtle glare. "I know it's like a mortal sin to cuss in front of an angel, but fuck, I just can't help it. I'm so fucking mad! And Peter, that little shit, he *knew* this was going to happen. He told me it was going to get worse before it gets better. Why couldn't he give me a heads up so maybe, just *maybe*, all of this could have been prevented? *Fuck!*" Lily collapsed back onto the bed after her fit of rage subsided.

"Are you done?"

Lily's head popped up, her glare fixed on her husband's raised brow. She propped herself up on her elbows as he sent her a glare of his own.

"Lil, I can't deny that this situation is completely cocked up. First, about the Becca and Ian thing…I'm sure he found her because he was looking for you, and who knows what she told him. What she *does* know, is that you left him with no intention of ever going back. That fact alone could have brought them together." He reached the bed, his fingers stroking the chilled flesh of her exposed shoulder. "This Liam character is some delusional little twit that will have to be put in his place, and who better to do that than us." He knelt beside the bed, his lips meeting her collarbone. "The whole dirty mouth is actually dead sexy. I'd like to see what you might say in a very different situation." Her head fell back as his tongue flicked across her hardened nipple.

She let out a soft moan as the heat began to radiate across her chest. Her fingers threaded into the hair at the nape of his neck and pulled. She brought his lips up to hers as his body took its place on top of hers.

"We...don't..." She tried to speak, but his tongue kept interfering with her ability.

After a moment, Ryan pulled back, his hand cupping at her cheek. "I love how I do this," he said, as his thumb caressed her warmed cheek. "But you're right, we need to get dressed and get your friends back."

"If Liam wants what I think he does, it's not going to be easy."

# Chapter Sixteen

## Trapped

*S*am sat in his translucent cage wearing only his dress shirt and slacks. He wasn't sure how his prison had been constructed or why it was actually containing him, but he knew there was something more powerful than himself at work. That fact alone terrified him.

A break in the stark white wall appeared and Liam walked through. Sam's eyes met his, but he wouldn't give him the respect of rising to meet him.

"Sammael, I see you've woken from your nap. How are you feeling?" Liam walked up to the barrier with his hands behind his back.

"Let's cut the crap, shall we? What do you want?" Sam rested his forearms on his raised knees.

"Cut to the chase, I see. Well, we are waiting for your friend, Lily, to arrive in Reading. Once she's put her cold little hands on the book I need, there will be an exchange."

"Exchange? You make it sound like a bank transaction. These are people's lives. What about Ian and Becca?"

"Don't worry, your precious companions are just fine. They are together, if that makes you feel any better."

Sam sighed and let his chin fall to his chest. Ever since he had awoken, his thoughts were in a million pieces as he feared any type of suffering Becca could be in. He had failed her in so many ways in her lifetime; he vowed this would not be another.

"When can I see them?"

"As soon as Lily and I make the exchange. Don't ask when that will be because I don't know at this point. I'll give you updates as soon as I have anything to report."

Liam left through the same break in the white wall as he had entered.

Sam's head fell backward and hit the wall of his cage, his eyes staring upward. "I sure hope you know what you're doing. I can't let Rebecca down – not again."

ʊ ᴡ ⱷ

Ian flexed his stiff fingers as his eyes fluttered open, his gaze following down his arm to notice what his fingers had between them. He could feel warm, soft flesh beneath the sheet. As his eyes moved up, he admired the black cotton sheet that barely covered the voluptuous breasts underneath. Once he reached her face, he saw an expression he was nowhere near prepared for. Even though the memories of being transported somehow and chained up were vague, he knew the situation they were in shouldn't be a happy one. Yet, Becca radiated complete contentment.

Her long dark lashes wavered just slightly as her eyes moved beneath their lids, her lips slightly parted, curved upward at the corners. Her hair was swept behind her in a loose ponytail, and his eyes followed the flowing strands to see the sheet was not covering most of her back; her scar plainly visible. His fingertips moved on instinct to trace the raised skin, and were honored with an unexpected moan.

Heat flushed throughout his body at the sound of Becca's unconscious vocals. He tried to move his hand, but for some reason he couldn't make himself – he was a man after all. His body was bound to react to a beautiful, mostly naked woman lying just inches from him. He wanted to chalk it up to his hormones, but he had a nagging feeling that was nowhere near what was happening.

He concentrated on why he was even in the situation he was in. Lily. Her smile, her laugh, her love... He'd come halfway around the world to find a woman he had wanted to spend the rest of his life with, after knowing her just a few months. That brought his thoughts to the reason why she left; her secret. She had run away from him, from her life in Boston, even from her own daughter. A sickening knot formed in his stomach at the realization that he hadn't really known Lily at all. She ran before he really had a chance.

He let his mind wander to why it was that Becca had even brought him with her. Becca wanted Lily's happiness more than anything, but at what cost? He knew how much Becca loved Lily, but what about her own happiness? After all she had been through, why wasn't it Lily who was running after Becca helping chase *her* happiness?

This brought up the question of what he had really seen in Lily to begin with. Was it just some vampiric spell or was it really her? Did she love him for who he was, or was he just acting like the man she wanted? His mind was swimming in questions and doubt, wondering if any of the months they spent together were real.

He swallowed hard as Becca's hand moved from grasping the sheet between her breasts to limply exploring what was around her. Once she found Ian's shoulder, she pulled herself close and snuggled onto his chest. He turned to lie on his back so her cheek would rest on his bare chest. Her hand snaked across his stomach to gently grasp at his hip.

He couldn't stop the thoughts of Becca racing through his mind. She was insanely smart as well as devastatingly beautiful. The first moment he saw her he felt something he knew he shouldn't. The whole reason for going through everything was for Lily, but after the pretense of being Becca's fiancé and finding out her horrific experience with Gideon, he couldn't help feeling closer to her than Lily. She seemed to trust him instantly. Admittedly, he felt the same or else he wouldn't have left his life to follow her halfway around the world. Even though his heartache had been excruciating in Lily's absence, he was starting to think it had all happened for a reason. Becca.

His thoughts of confusion about his feelings for Lily and Becca were interrupted when he heard the door on the other side of the room open. Liam walked in and closed the door behind him before making his way over to Becca's side of the bed.

Ian held onto Becca tighter as he saw the disgusting gleam in Liam's eyes as he took in the view of her backside.

"She's so beautiful while she's sleeping, don't you think?" Liam raised his gaze to focus on Ian.

"I hope she can sleep through this entire ordeal." Ian uttered quietly through clenched teeth.

"I don't think she can sleep that long. The preparations that need to be made might take a while." Liam's fingertips grazed Becca's spine.

Ian's muscles tensed as he pulled at his chains while attempting to pull Becca in closer.

Liam softly laughed as he pulled back from the bedside. "I thought Lily was the one you were after?"

"We were looking for her. We both need answers."

"If things go as planned, we will all get them." Liam made his way towards the door before Ian called out.

"Hey, is Lily coming? What about clothes and food and a bathroom? Where is Sam? Why isn't he in here?"

Liam turned back towards the bed with a disturbing grin. "Lily will come and we will make an exchange. Once Becca is awake and I can trust the both of you, you'll be released from the chains and brought food – no clothes I'm afraid. As for Sam," he rubbed at the back of his neck while letting out a short chuckle. "I don't think it would be very appropriate for him to see the two of you like this. He also needs a different sort of confinement given his special abilities."

With another snarky chuckle, he left Ian with Becca in his arms wondering exactly what the hell was going on.

ଞ ᰒ ଛ

Becca slept for a few more hours in Ian's arms as he contemplated all the ways they could get themselves out of the predicament they were in. Unfortunately, Ian had no clue what to do. He had just about given up on the thoughts of escape when Becca began to stir.

She felt her brain throbbing in her skull as she peeled her cheek from the warm skin it had been stuck to. Her eyes blinked slowly, her surroundings blurry and barely distinguishable. She felt the tug at her wrist as she lifted herself up, seeing she was cuffed to something and the sheet slipped lower as she became upright. Her eyes shut tightly for a few seconds so she could attempt to clear the film that had gathered over them. Once she opened them again, things were much clearer. She was staring at Ian lying barechested, with a sheet that covered just above his hips.

She looked again up to where her wrist was cuffed and discovered Ian had his wrist cuffed also. She looked back down at Ian who had a very concentrated look on his face, staring straight into her eyes. His breathing was labored as he attempted to sit up next to her. A sudden wave of nausea overtook her before he could get that far.

"I'm gonna' puke!" She turned, frantically swinging her legs off the side of the bed while her arm stretched and the dry heaves began.

"Just a sec. Shit!"

She felt him move behind her on the bed as she tried to swallow down what was attempting to rise.

"Here!" He thrust a pillowcase into her hands.

She opened it just seconds before she let go. What little she had eaten over the past twenty-four hours spilled out until there was nothing left. Ian's hand held her hair at the nape of her neck, making sure to keep it from getting doused in the mess spewing from her mouth.

Once she felt she was done, she took several deep breaths and took in her surroundings.

"Where are we?"

Ian rested his head on the back of her shoulder as he took a few cleansing breaths of his own.

"I don't know. Liam came in a few hours ago and said some bullshit about making an exchange with Lily. He seems to think she'll come after us. He says Sam is safe, but won't be with us. Considering the way we're being kept, I think that might be a good idea."

Ian lifted his head, his breath trailing down Becca's spine. Pinpricks of heat spiked in each of her vertebrae, a fluid warmth possessing her body.

The second she turned to look at him was when she realized she was only wearing underwear, and looked down to see a tiny pair of black lace boy shorts clinging to her hips. She yanked the sheet up to cover her breasts, and then covered her face as the tears begin to flow.

"No, no, it's okay. I know it doesn't look that way right now, but-"

Becca cut him off with the sharp rise of her head. "It's not okay!" She brought the sheet up to her eyes to wipe her tears. "We have no idea where we are, no idea how we got here. We are cuffed to a headboard, half-naked..." She let out another sob before continuing. "And I don't know about you, but these were *not* the undergarments I was wearing the last time I was conscious."

"I'm going to *kill* that fucker! He was-"

"Oh, don't worry. That little shit is going to get his."

That was the moment Liam decided to greet his newly awakened detainee.

"I wouldn't say such things, if I were you. I've come to help."

Liam brought boxes of supplies in on a hand cart from the hallway.

"I've got bottled water and some food. Some hygiene products and a portable toilet complete with tissues. That should hold you for a while."

"What about clothes?!" Becca shouted.

Liam's sickly smile spread across his lips. "As I explained to Mr. Holt earlier, you will be allowed your undergarments only while you are here. Less chance of escape, even if you could."

"Becca's sick, she needs medication," Ian pleaded.

"I'll see if I have anything for nausea. Maybe try to sip some water and I'll be back to check on you later." Liam turned toward the door.

"Wait!" Becca practically cried. "What about the cuffs and the pillowcase full of puke?"

Liam came back to the bedside to retrieve the soiled pillowcase and looked into Becca's eyes as he picked it up. He took it and placed it just outside the door before returning to Becca's side of the bed.

"I will let you out on the condition that you not get yourself into trouble. I know how that brilliant mind of yours works, Agent Swift, but there is no escape. There are forces here that you are nowhere near capable of challenging. I will keep you both as comfortable as possible. In return, you will do as I say until it is time for the exchange to be made." Liam released Becca's wrist from her cuff before bringing his hand up to cup at her cheek. "I'm not a monster, Becca. Well, at least...not yet."

He silently made his way over to release Ian from his cuff. Becca shook her head for Ian to know not to make a move.

"I'll be back shortly." He shut the door and a foreign clicking sound rang throughout the room.

"Game plan?" Ian asked, as he flopped back onto the bed.

Becca slowly lay herself down next to him, her hand clutching the sheet in between her breasts.

"I don't think we're getting out of here. That sound?" She turned her head to him.

His eyes turned to meet hers. "Yeah?"

"I'm pretty sure that was a Tersuline lock. It's the kind of lock that's used to keep something, or in this case, some*one* in, with no way of breaking out," She sighed, as she let her eyelids slide shut.

"Hey." Ian's palm caressed at her cheek until she opened her eyes again. "Lily's coming. She'll get us out."

"I'm not sure even she can help us out of this." Becca's chest tightened at the thought of possibly losing Lily once and for all.

## Chapter Seventeen

## Leatherby Manor

When they arrived on the doorstep of the only place Lily had really ever called home, an instant chill seared through her; she knew this visit would not be a pleasant one.

Lily maneuvered the lock and opened the ornate wooden door. The four of them piled into the foyer, their rain drenched clothes dripping all over the dust covered floor.

"This is it – home sweet home. Welcome to Leatherby Manor." Lily's arm swept over the space that she hadn't seen in over five years.

"Wow." Renee spun around slowly while looking to the two story ceiling. "I can't believe you stay in that tiny cabin when you could be living *here*. This is amazing."

"Lots of memories, I guess." Lily looked over to a few framed photos that still adorned the wall. She brought her fingertips to the glass, removing the grime to discover what lay beneath.

Ryan came up behind Lily and placed his hands on her hips. "Is that him?"

"Yeah, that's Martin." If Lily could cry, she was sure her eyes would be full to the brim. Her chest ached as she gazed at one of the last pictures taken of Martin.

He stood tall in one of his favorite spots of Ormeau Park in Belfast, Ireland. It was just after sunset and his usually perfect brown hair was blowing wildly in the wind. His chocolate colored eyes and gleaming white teeth only accentuated his ruggedly handsome presence. He looked as vibrant as he always did, not the defeated man he became in the last days of his existence.

Lily shook off her memories as Ryan's arms slipped around her waist to clasp in front of her.

"Where are these books hidden? The Library?" Abe questioned, as he made his move for the monstrous staircase.

"No. We have to go down." She made her way to the hall closet and found the box she was looking for straight away. "If you want to come with me, you're going to need these." She pulled a few lanterns out of the box and proceeded to light them.

Ryan took one as she handed the other to Abe.

"It can be a tight fit down there, just try to stay close together."

Lily walked further into the house and disengaged a panel underneath the stairs. They all had to stoop to enter the seemingly endless spiral stairwell.

"How many steps are there?" Renee huffed after about five minutes into their decent.

"Just about there." Lily called over her shoulder.

Two minutes and a few hundred steps later, they arrived at a thick paneled door. Lily took the lantern from Ryan and brought it up to the hand carved cabinet just beside the doorknob.

She pressed her hand on the face of the cabinet. It opened slightly before Lily pulled it open the rest of the way, to reveal a small cylinder embedded into the stone wall inside.

Lily looked to each of her three companions silently before she slipped her right index finger into the cylinder.

The finger glided past a glass barrier with little force. A carbon steel blade met the tip to slice through the skin and blood began to drip into the small divot below. Screeching of gears and grinding of steel on steel, the door began to unlock from its confines.

Lily carefully removed her finger and brought it to her lips, letting the venom coat the cut on her fingertip to heal it almost instantly.

"It's a chemical lock. It can only be opened with my blood," Lily shrugged, as the rest stood about slightly stunned. "I have a Master's in Chemistry. I did use it for a few things."

"There is so much we need to catch up on." Ryan patted the curve of Lily's back as she pried the door open.

Lily led the way into a large room with walls reaching two stories, all covered in books.

"Well, this should be fun," Abe quipped.

Lily turned to send a glare in his direction.

"So, you know exactly where this book is that we're looking for?" Abe raised his eyebrows and pursed his lips in question.

"I have a general idea. It's not like these are things that can be cataloged alphabetically. Some are in languages that haven't been spoken in thousands of years. I don't think the Dewey Decimal system would apply." Lily set her lantern on the table situated in the middle of the room.

"Does that work?" Renee pointed upward to the chandelier precariously hanging above them.

"Let's find out." Lily found the electrical box on the wall. A flip of a switch, a whir of the generator, and the underground library was completely illuminated.

Lily found her way over to the library ladder while Abe and Renee settled down in the chairs at the table. Lily climbed a third of the way up the ladder to reach the bar to move it along the wall. Ryan stood at the bottom as she moved herself along.

"Hope you've got strong arms, 'cause you're gonna need them." Lily plucked out the first book and tossed it down to him below.

Ryan grunted and his knees almost gave out from beneath him as the weight of the book fell into his arms.

"That's just volume one."

ৼ ᛁ ৶

Lily had retrieved all of the books she thought they would need. The stacks were piled high on the table, obstructing their views of each other.

"Have you actually read this book before?" Abe scratched at his forehead as he searched through the yellowing pages.

"Abe, let's not get into this now." Lily sighed.

Abe stood up to peer over the books at her. "When Lil? When we find Becca dead because we couldn't figure out what language the fucking 'turn-me-into-a-vampire' ritual is in?"

Lily moved at lightening speed to Abe, grabbing him by the throat before throwing him to the floor. She held him there as she added her knee, pressing down on his chest.

"Don't you *ever* imply that I don't care about her! She's my daughter; I would do anything for her!"

"You don't think I would?" Abe choked out with the little breath he had. "I love her too."

Ryan's hand on Lily's shoulder brought her out of her rage. She pushed herself off Abe's chest before dusting herself off.

Lily turned her head as she heard sniffling beside her and found Renee wiping her eyes with the cuff of her shirt.

"Oh, shit. I'm sorry." Lily rushed over to Renee. "I didn't mean to scare you."

"No." Renee shook her head as Lily took her by the hand. "That's not it." She wiped her eyes once again and took a deep breath. "You both love her so much. It just makes it that much more real, ya know?"

Lily turned to see Abe with his arms tight around his chest. She squeezed her eyes tight before turning back to Renee and focusing on what needed to be said.

"I know this is all new to you. We just need to try to get through this so we can get them back as soon as possible. I promise when this is over, you, me, and Becca will all sit down and have and nice long talk about all this. Alright?"

Lily stroked her fingertips through the wisps of hair that had fallen out of Renee's ponytail. Renee nodded as she looked into Lily's sincere eyes.

"Let's get back to it then." Lily and Abe once again exchanged glares as the four of them settled back down at the table.

ᚷ ᚹ ᛉ

"This is all chicken scratch to me. This one even looks like a tiny bird walked all over the page," Renee huffed, as she slid the large book across the table then slumped back in her chair.

Abe caught a glimpse of the book before reaching for the delicately preserved pages. His eyes raked over the symbols, some familiar, some not. When he recognized a symbol he knew was pertinent to what they were looking for, he finally spoke up.

"Lil? How is your Sumerian?"

She raised an eyebrow at him as he lifted the book to display the page he was looking at.

"I studied it a while back at the British Museum. This is more recent though." Lily's fingertip traced the familiar symbols. "Hellenistic period, maybe?"

"It would fit the time period we're looking for." Abe leaned across the table to look at what Lily was scanning. "You think you can translate it?"

"Yeah, just give me a minute."

Lily's brain went into retrieval mode. She crept through the corners of her mind to retrieve the information she desperately needed. She remembered the nights spent with Martin going over his history and that of his sire. Martin had been a British warrior, turned in the eleventh century during the Crusades. His sire, Lior, had been an Ahbmonite, turned into a vampire only because that is what every generation before him had done. Lior had passed down many books to Martin, and Martin in turn, had passed them on to Lily.

Armed with her memories and education, Lily began to translate the ancient text. Within an hour, she had a rough idea of what needed to be said and done.

The grumbling of Renee's stomach brought her out of her head and back to the three sitting at the table with her.

"I think I've got a good idea of what to do." She sat back in her chair as she raked her fingers roughly through her hair. "Why don't we make our way back up and see if we can find something for Renee to eat before her stomach starts digesting itself."

Lily gathered up the book she needed as Abe and Ryan returned the others to their rightful shelves.

"You think this is what you need to help Becca?" Renee whispered, as she and Lily made their way toward the door.

"I hope so." Lily went over to the cabinet inside the room. She retrieved another piece of glass to replace the one she had destroyed while unlocking the room. She cleared the broken glass, and then slid the new pane in.

"I can hardly believe all of this. Locks that open with blood, ancient dead languages, vampires, demons..." Renee hooked her arm through Lily's and rested her head on her shoulder.

"Don't forget the angels."

"Yep," Renee sighed, as she looked over to Abe and Ryan. "Them too."

Renee's stomach made another demand for food, rather loudly.

"Can't Abe just poof us up? I don't think I can handle those stairs again."

"No can do. Martin was very protective of this place. He had a dampening field placed down here. No 'poofing' allowed, sorry."

Renee let out a soft pout as Lily led her out to the bottom of the stairs. Ryan and Abe followed before Lily carefully shut and locked the door once again.

Half the way up the stairs, Renee was huffing and puffing and Abe graciously offered to carry her the rest of the way. Her cheeks reddened a little from both exertion and embarrassment, but she accepted his offer.

Once back up in the foyer, Lily heard a rustling noise coming from the back of the house.

"It's just me, old girl. Come and bring your friends in here for a cup of tea."

Lily sighed in relief at Jefferson's voice floating in from the kitchen and followed his voice, anxious for a cup of tea.

Lily walked into a sight she had never seen in her kitchen – a tea kettle on the stove warming, an assortment of cakes and scones on a tray, as well as bread and cheese ready to be sliced.

"Jefferson, you've outdone yourself. I thought you wouldn't come until tomorrow?" Lily went over the young man with light brown hair and soft green eyes, giving him a big hug that ended with a sloppy kiss on the cheek.

"Well, when you mentioned friends coming with you, I realized they were most likely of the human variety and would need a little something to fill their bellies."

"Yes." Renee stuffed a scone in her mouth. "So good." She chewed ravenously, before gulping down a nearby cup of tea.

"Guess I was right," Jefferson laughed, the apron tied around his waist swishing with each breath.

Lily made all of the necessary introductions as they gathered around the table to settle in for their meal.

"When was the last time you fed?" Ryan whispered into Lily's ear, while slipping his arm around the back of her chair.

"A while," she sighed, her own hunger gnawing on her insides.

"Don't worry old girl. I didn't forget you." Jefferson brought over a large mug of crimson liquid. "Our favorite butcher was glad to hear one of his best customers was coming back to town."

"Thank you." Lily sipped the blood at first, in an attempt to be polite but once the sustenance flowed down her throat she gulped it down.

She slammed her mug down once she had drained every last drop from the mug.

"Sorry." She licked her lips to remove any remaining traces of pig blood.

"So, what now?" Abe asked, before stuffing a large vanilla cake in his mouth.

Lily took a deep breath as she surveyed the table. "We wait."

# Chapter Eighteen

## Realization

"There's a lot you're not telling me, isn't there?" Ian sat back against the headboard as Becca paced in front of him with the sheet wrapped tightly around her.

"There is no way I can tell you everything. I wouldn't even know where to begin..." She bit down on her thumbnail as she turned to make another pass across the room.

"You tell me then, how should we be looking at this? Should we be using your FBI skills or should we work with what you know from your time at Manchester?" He raised his brow as she finally stopped to look at him.

"Manchester, definitely. Certain people in the FBI know about these things but it wasn't like we were trained on ways to banish a demon or how to summon..." she cut off mid-sentence and froze.

"What?" Ian jumped up anxiously to her side.

She turned toward him, and his hands instinctively went to rest on her hips. "Peter. I can try and summon Peter."

"He's an angel, right?"

"Not just an angel." She looked deep into his eyes and smiled. "He's *the* right hand."

"What do we do? Chant or something?"

"Um, no." She felt her breath coming out in soft pants as she realized they were pressed tightly against each other. "I just have to concentrate. I've only done it once before and it was with Lily."

She backed away from Ian's embrace and his arms fell to his sides. She immediately felt the loss of their connection and was wondering if he did too.

Becca went back over to the bed and made herself comfortable. She closed her eyes and took a few deep breaths as she lay as still as possible.

"Can I try too?" The bed dipped just a bit as Ian came to lie at her side.

"Sure." She kept her eyes closed and despite Ian's proximity, she was able to keep her breathing calm.

*Peter. Peter. Peter. Peter. Peter.*

Over and over she visualized him in her mind, concentrating on her memories of his face. His shaggy brown hair and crystal clear, blue eyes, his smile, his presence... She remembered what it felt like to be near him, the connection and the feeling of rightness.

While Becca concentrated on contacting Peter, Ian concentrated on Becca.

Ian thought about how his whole life had been planned and scheduled up to the last detail until he graduated from the conservatory. Who his friends were, what schools he attended, how he would dress... He was his parent's only child and there was nothing they wouldn't do for a Holt legacy.

Ian's mother, Marian, encouraged his music when he was a child. She made sure he had the finest teachers and the best piano to study on. She didn't realize that her encouragement would pull him away from his expected path to honor and glory. In her mind's eye, she saw him on the Senate floor right next to his father, Bradford, helping lead the country into the next age. But instead of studying law at Northwestern with his football scholarship, he decided to attend the Boston Conservatory. Marion was enraged, Bradford was proud. It was a subject his parents had fought endlessly over. Bradford had been an outstanding prosecutor in his younger years and always knew how to win an argument, so most of them ended in his favor.

When Marian realized she was fighting a losing battle, she gave up that fight and took up another one – finding Ian a wife. Every decent looking woman in Ian's age range that was a registered Democrat was paraded in front of him. Ian admitted to himself he had been somewhat of a player at one time, but he was never serious about any of them. He certainly had never been in love.

The night he met Lily, he had been having an inner debate on the way he had been living his life. He loved women and knew what amazing sex felt like, but he'd never had that connection that people wrote about in love songs. Ian had no one to share his accomplishments with. No one to share a life with, like his parents had always shared theirs.

Lily was a breath of fresh air. She wasn't from any political circle, yet she was accomplished and wealthy in her own right. She could hold her own in any argument and she most definitely challenged him in the bedroom. She was a perfect fit, yet there was something missing. Something he didn't even realize until Becca came into his life. Where Lily brought excitement and challenges to his life, Becca felt like his best friend.

The night Becca told him about Lily and the world they lived in, his first instinct was to jump in head first. He blamed his desperate need for Lily on love, when in reality he never knew what it was. Just talking to Becca about her life and the way she had lived, he felt a more intrinsic connection with her in hours than he had in months with Lily. After visiting The Manchester Group and learning Becca's horrific story, he began to let his mind wander.

He began to work on a theory of why Lily had chosen the path she had. Not only was she attempting to save him from danger, but herself as well. He thought that until he had entered her life, Lily's only purpose for being was Becca. Then he came in, swept her off her feet and messed everything up. He caused her to go against a vow she'd kept to her husband for so long and her core nature of how she lived her life. He came to believe Lily's life had a purpose and he was never intended to be a part of it.

Now, lying next to Becca, listening to her even breaths, he just knew she was the reason his life had taken the turns it had. Every step in his life had led him to the moment he would find his other half. He had fought it at first; after all, Lily had been his soul reason for living for months. But that desperation is what led him to Becca and he knew he couldn't waste another of the few precious moments they might have left without telling her how he felt and hope that their futures lay together.

"I don't think this is working." Ian pulled Becca out of her concentrated gaze as he turned onto his side.

"It hasn't been that long. Just keep trying," Becca huffed, and closed her eyes tighter.

"I know time is an odd concept in this place, but I think it's been at least a few hours. I think we need to talk about something else." Ian rested his hand on her covered stomach.

Her breath hitched as the warmth of his hand flowed to the center of her body. "What-" She attempted to clear her throat to control her thoughts from turning down a road she thought they should never go down. "What did you have in mind?"

"I think I should get one thing out of the way first. I think I understand Lily a little better now. What I mean is, her motivations for living the way she does."

Becca nodded silently for him to go on.

"The reason she never had a relationship was because she could never let go of Ryan. I think maybe being with me was just a fluke. She tried to believe that we were what each other needed and ran away from it to protect both of us. I think maybe her mission in life is to protect you and do what she needs to do to move on to the next life – a life where she can be with Ryan again."

Becca wiped a tear that had traitorously escaped onto her cheek. "You're right," she sniffled. "At least about her. Until she met you, she never even talked about a romantic relationship. I think it was literally hell on earth for her the day we had the sex talk. If she could have blushed, she would have been a tomato." Becca laughed at the memory of Lily supplying her with a pint of chocolate-chip cookie dough ice cream while the talk of the birds and the bees was attempted. "I could tell she was lonely, but whenever she got too down she asked for another assignment and we were off to help someone else in a new part of the world."

"You didn't mind all the globetrotting?" Ian let his index finger lightly trial up and down her stomach.

"No, I mean yes... sometimes. I was a moody teenager at times, but once I realized what we were really doing, how we were helping, I learned that it was what we were both born to do."

He knew the next question had to be asked, but he didn't really want to know the answer. "And how did Abe figure into the life you were meant to lead?"

"He...he was what made it all worth it, for a while at least. I used to joke with him that he was my reward from Peter, or whoever runs things up there for all my hard work," she huffed, as she held the sheet tight to her chest. "You know how well that worked out."

"Yeah, but he really loved you; still does as far as I could see."

"I know, but..." she turned over on her side to face him, his hand slid to rest on her hip. "I just can't."

"I know that even if we do get out of here, after everything I know now, my future lies here." He brought his hand up to lie gently over her heart. "It took meeting a vampire to help me find the human I think I was always meant to be with."

"Ian..." Becca sighed his name in a whisper.

"Just let me get this out." He gently ran his fingertip from just above her heart to underneath her chin. "Lily was excitement and adrenalin –

something I thought I needed to survive. When I lost it, I was desperate to get it back. But the first night you and I met, after a while Lily was the furthest thing from my mind. I wanted to know you, everything about you. I tried to fight it, concentrate on what we set out to do, but I can't anymore. Please don't tell me I'm making a total ass out of myself."

She let out a soft laugh as she gently closed her eyes. "The whole reason I came to you was to help Lily." She opened her eyes to find his face mere inches away, his breath mingling with her own. She brought her hand to rest on his hip. "I can't deny that it has been a very long time since I felt like this. I just didn't want to let myself hope."

"You want this? You want me?" he asked, his fingertip caressing her bottom lip.

"Yes," she whispered, as her eyes darted down to his lips.

He pressed his lips lightly to hers before pulling back, leaving a wisp of space between them.

"That's all I get?" She smiled as her heart skipped a few beats, her hand trembling as she brought it up to rest on his cheek.

"No," he laughed softly against her lips. "I just don't want to get too carried away. We don't know who might be watching and if you keep panting the way you are, I might very well not give a fuck and take you right here."

Becca let out a long, delicious moan as heat pulsed throughout her lower body. She hitched her leg over his hip before attacking his lips with a fervor she had never possessed before.

He responded with the same passion, pulling her on top of him, groaning at the warmth her contact caused across his skin. He let his body just feel for once – there were no consequences, no tomorrow, only that moment to touch and caress and desire what he had been waiting for his entire life.

"Ian," she sighed, as his hand made its way between the lace and the skin of her backside.

"I can't stop. I want you too much." His other hand gently caressed the side of her breast that was pressed against his bare chest.

"Pull the covers over us," she whispered as she nipped at his neck. "If they are watching, we're not going to give them a free show."

He rolled her off of him and they dug their way under the covers and back into each other's arms.

"Now, where were we?" Ian asked with a quirked brow.

Becca took his hand and brought it down to her backside. "Right about here, I think."

"Not quite." He softly pecked her lips before he slipped his hand beneath the lace. "Yes, right here I think." He gave her flesh a little squeeze before he brought his lips back to hers.

Mere seconds into their undercover make out session, they heard the Tersuline lock open and they froze as the door opened then closed. They both carefully peeked up from under the cover to find Liam standing with a smirk on his face.

"You leave us alone for hours on end and this is the moment you decide to interrupt?" Becca let her head fall back on the pillow in frustration.

"It's time," Liam answered.

Becca looked a little more closely to notice Liam was holding a bag in his left hand.

"Becca, it's time to get dressed and say goodbye to your friend." Becca shot up to sit in bed, but her protests were cut off. "Not forever, just for a little while. From what I've just witnessed, Mr. Holt will be a big part of our future plans." Liam dropped the bag and turned to leave. "Ten minutes."

The sound of the door locking signaled the end of the shortest chapter of Becca's life.

"I promise, I'll figure away to get back to you. If Lily is here, I know she will overtake that little shit and we will be out of here in no time."

Ian brought her back into his arms. "I hope it is all true, but if we never find each other again, please know that even in this fucked up mess were in, you are it for me."

Becca pulled him in for one long, tongue-tangling, teeth-gnashing, lip-burning kiss.

Tears began to stream down both of their cheeks as they softly brought their kiss to an end.

Becca jumped up, grabbed the bag and ripped it open before dumping out the contents. A pair of socks, some running shoes, jeans, a long sleeved t-shirt, and a bra that matched the panties she was already wearing. She dressed herself in a hurry, not looking back at Ian once.

She had just finished tying her shoelaces when the lock turned again.

Liam stood in the open doorway and offered his hand to her.

Becca took a deep breath and looked back to the bed one last time. The pain and terror in Ian's eyes clawed at her heart. She knew how scared he must be, but she had to see whatever plan Liam had, just until she found Lily.

A tear slipped down her cheek as she mouthed, "I promise".

He nodded his head in recognition before she turned back to face Liam.

She swatted his hand out of the way and passed by him into the blackened hall. The door shut quickly behind them and she was thrust into darkness.

A sudden light flickered on and she blinked to see what was before her.

Terrified, the word barely made it passed her lips. "You?"

She felt a sharp pain in her back and fell to the floor before spiraling into an unknown darkness, not knowing when or if she would wake again.

## Chapter Nineteen

## Best Laid Plans

*H*is Adam's apple bobbed as he brought his hand to knock on the door to the illusive **Leatherby Manor** in the dark of night. His fist scrunched tight as he banged against the hard wood. Within just a moment, Jefferson stood before him.

"Yes, boy?"

"I was told to deliver this to the lady of the house." The young boy of twelve shook slightly as he produced the thick envelope that had been hiding under his overcoat.

"I will see she gets it." Jefferson held his hand out for the envelope, but the boy pulled back.

"No, sir. I was told to deliver it to the lady of the house and no one else. I need to hand it directly to Mrs. Lily Edwards." His voice shook up and down as he attempted to make his stance.

"Alright, then." Jefferson ducked his head back inside and yelled. "Old girl! There's a young lad here for ya."

Slight footsteps were heard as Lily made her way to the front door. She opened the door a bit wider to see the boy standing on her doorstep.

"Mrs. Edwards?" the boy asked as he let out a sigh.

"Yes, that's me." Lily smiled down at the boy who appeared to be frightened to death.

"Here." He thrust the envelope into her hands and took off down the drive without another word.

He ran as hard and as fast as he could until he reached his destination several blocks away. He stood by the building of stone and mortar and waited for his payment to come.

"Did you see her?"

The boy stumbled, almost falling to the ground as the voice poured from the shadows.

"Ye-ye-yes, sir." His breath labored just as hard as his heart at that moment.

"Good. Very good." A deep maniacal laughter echoed off the stone walls sending a chill deep into the young boy's bones. "Your payment is behind the brick on the corner there, twelfth from the bottom." A loud swooshing sound and the voice retreated into the fog from which it came.

The boy made his way to the twelfth brick and collected his payment while vowing to himself never to talk to strangers again.

♌ ♈ ♉

Jefferson followed Lily into the living room after shutting the front door.

"You need any help reading that?" Jefferson eyed her as she sat down on the enormous couch.

"No. I think this is something I need to do on my own. Don't wake the others, they've had a long day."

"Sure." Jefferson gave Lily a kiss on the forehead before he made his way into the kitchen.

Lily slowly tore the envelope open and retrieved the pages that lay inside. She withdrew several pages of building schematics with certain rooms marked in red. She looked them over carefully before reading the letter that arrived with them.

*Lily,*

*By now, my love, you know what I have done. My only reason for doing any of this was to get your attention. You know what we both are and that we belong together. I know you felt it when I found you in Las Vegas. You can't deny our physical and chemical chemistry; this was meant to happen.*

*Follow the maps I have included and your friends will be set free with little to no harm done. I will give you until sunset. Don't disappoint me.*

*Yours for eternity,*
*Liam.*

Lily took a deep breath before returning to the schematics. She studied them religiously until the sun rose, awakening the rest of the house.

"No sleep again?" Ryan kissed the top of her head before noticing what she was looking at.

"I've had a few things on my mind." She handed him the letter from Liam and returned to her studies.

"This guy is completely mental." Ryan threw the letter back on the table and took a seat next to Lily.

"I know he is, but I just can't explain it. In Vegas, it was like some sort of magnetic connection. I couldn't help but be drawn to him. I'm just thankful I had the power within me to run away."

Ryan brought his arm around her shoulders and held her tight to his chest. "We *will* get them back."

"I have a plan." Lily pulled back to see her husband's gleaming smile.

"Of course you do."

"We will need Abe, but I think between the three of us, we can pull it off."

Lily was purposely being evasive. She couldn't let Ryan know what would ultimately happen if she wasn't strong enough to resist the pull Liam had on her. The small pieces of metal and plastic embedded in her spine had more than one purpose. If Lily attempted to change Liam, she knew without a doubt the chip would activate and life as she knew it would cease to exist.

ଛ ଔ ଷ

Late afternoon approached as they went over Lily's plan for the fiftieth time.

"I get it, already." Abe threw his hands up and leaned back in his chair, the wooden legs groaning in the process.

"We just have to make sure we are all on the same page. I know right now he's human, but we all agree he's had help on this. We don't know what kind of traps he could have laid out for us," Lily replied, as she pulled at the ends of her hair. She knew she had been stalling for hours, but she had to make sure they did everything the way she had laid out.

"We're ready then." Ryan stood and offered his hand out to Lily.

Lily got up and held him in her arms as tight as she possibly could without breaking him.

"Jefferson and I will have the blood and food ready for all of you when you get back." Renee smiled over at Lily and Ryan with watery eyes.

Lily left Ryan's arms for Renee's. "I'm so sorry I got you involved in this."

"Are you kidding? This is the scariest fun I've ever had." They both giggled as they held each other tight.

"I cherish you. Never forget that." Lily slipped the keys to her cabin in Renee's pocket out of Ryan and Abe's sight.

Renee pulled back and nodded in acknowledgment of Lily's gift. She shed a few more silent tears as she and Abe hugged goodbye while Lily turned to Jefferson.

"You have that coffee that Becca loves?"

"Yes, don't worry. I have all of her favorites. They will be ready when you all set foot on the doorstep." Jefferson patted Lily's backside as she gathered the books she needed. "Now, go bring the family home."

Lily, Ryan, and Abe stepped out the front door and quietly closed it behind them.

Jefferson put his arm around Renee's shoulders and kissed her temple.

"She's not going to make it back, is she?"

Jefferson sighed as a tear slipped down his cheek. "No, I don't think she is."

# Chapter Twenty
## Moment Of Truth

Lily stepped with caution as the three of them arrived at their final destination.

The air was frozen, as if being held in place. There was not a sign of life anywhere – no birds flying or chirping, no creatures scampering about. The atmosphere was dead in every respect. That fact alone gave another edge to the multifaceted sword.

The ground was crisp beneath their feet as they approached the lone building. It was an odd setting for an industrial warehouse in the middle of nowhere, but Lily thought that was possibly the exact appeal Liam was looking for.

"I know we've gone over this a million times, but once more please?" Lily looked to a solemn Ryan and an anxious Abe for their understanding.

"Go ahead," Ryan whispered with a kiss to the temple as Abe nodded, shifting from one foot to the other.

"I go through the south entrance there," Lily stated, pointing to the entrance straight in front of them. "Abe, can you tell if there is a protection field?"

Abe squeezed his eyes tight while taking a deep breath. "Definitely. That bastard isn't working alone on this one. The hold he's placed here...I haven't seen it in decades."

That did nothing for Lily's confidence. If Liam wasn't working alone, there was no guarantee her plans would work.

"Then the original plan stands. Abe, try the second story entrance on the west and Ryan will try the loading dock on the east end." Lily swallowed hard as the two men nodded in agreement.

She adjusted the strap of the bag across her torso before she was crushed into her husband's arms.

"I cannot tell you enough how much I love you. Be careful."

Lily's chest ached more in that moment than it did when her body was breaking, falling down that hill those many years ago. She knew she had to do whatever it took to keep her daughter safe. If that meant making the ultimate sacrifice, she prayed Ryan would understand.

"I will. I love you, always." She reached his lips with hers and gave every ounce of herself that she could in that moment.

"I think it's time," Abe grumbled, while kicking at the rocks on the ground.

They all nodded their acknowledgment and went their separate ways to face the fate that awaited each of them.

 R W S

Lily knew that she might have sent her angels on a wild goose chase, but she needed them close by just in case.

Each step she took brought her closer to what she needed most. The pull was even stronger than what she had felt in Las Vegas, something she hadn't accounted for. She had taken only a sip back then, but in that very moment her throat burned with the irrational hope that she would soon be drowning in his crimson delight.

She tried to shake off the monstrous desires and concentrate on releasing her friends, yet the closer she got to where she knew he would be, the ability to reign herself in reached an epic threat she'd never experienced before.

The first thing she noticed when she entered the room was the blade held at the jugular vein of her daughter. Liam had Becca's hands and ankles tied down to the steel chair in the center of the blackened room.

Lily kept her distance, for fear that any movement she made would make his hand slip, causing the blade to torment Becca further. She could see he was enjoying the emotions seeping into the room; hate, fear, and unfortunate desire exuded from her every fiber. His exhilaration traveled swiftly through him as he reveled in looming over Becca. The tip of his knife caressed the thin sheet of skin that covered her vein, as his tongue slipped across to moisten his more than perfect lips.

The blade caught a tear from Becca's cheek before it had a chance to fall; its taste divine as he wiped the blade across his tongue, stimulating each taste bud.

"Time is running out. Blood will be spilt whatever you decide, you need only to choose whose it will be."

Lily had a choice to make. She knew she had only moments before he would carry out every threat he had promised to. His one demand was the only thing holding her back.

She took one last long look over him. His eyes, still the same deep blue piercing through her from within the shadows; his smile, still just as perfectly charming. When she looked deeper, however, she saw something in him more clearly than she ever had before; his soul. Black and corrupted by words she was sure he himself almost certainly didn't comprehend.

Her eyes narrowed and her jaw clenched. She tried with everything she possessed to fight the hunger tearing inside of her. "They will kill me if I do this." Her words were resolute, but her voice was trembling at the incredulous truth of it all.

"Then you have a decision to make. Whose existence is more important?" He brought his cheek next to Becca's, sealing a tear upon it with a kiss. "Hers or your own...?"

Before he could let the last breath pass through his lips, she replied. "Hers."

Becca whimpered from beneath her cloth gag while struggling with her bindings. Her tears came in longer streams, her breaths in pants as she saw Lily produce a large book from the bag on her shoulder.

"Are you sure?" Lily pleaded one last time for him to run away as the burning within her began to attack every inch of her skin.

"Yes." His voice was hard and absolutely certain.

Lily swallowed the venom that flowed freely into her mouth as she opened the book to the passage she would need for their binding ceremony.

Lily set the book on the floor beside her before crooking her finger and beckoning her final meal in front of her.

Liam swiftly pocketed his blade and went to stand before the woman that would bring him eternal life.

Lily slowly circled him before whispering the words of the quartet of ancestors. She tried to keep her eyes away from her daughter as her hands roamed the planes of Liam's torso. The bitter battle raged between her mind, her voice, and her body. Her mind screamed for her to stop, to grab Becca, and run faster than she ever had before while her voice echoed the words of honor and glory for a race forgotten for decades. But her body convulsed slightly in delight as she journeyed closer to her personal vampiric nirvāna.

The final words left her lips as her front pressed firmly to his backside. She took one final look at her daughter. Becca cried, screamed, and fought with everything she had left in her but she couldn't stop what happened next.

Lily sunk her teeth deep into the jugular vein that had been calling to her inner demon since that fateful day in Vegas. The blood slipped seamlessly down her throat, filling her with a euphoria nothing in the entire universe could be compared to.

Liam twitched in pain as he fell to his knees, but Lily would not yield. Her teeth stayed cemented into his flesh as almost every drop was drained and replaced with the venom from the only female vampire in existence.

Soon, his twitches of pain gave way to moans of pleasure. Liam's panting breaths came quick and hard as his body gave in to the change.

Lily's teeth ripped the flesh from Liam's neck as the excruciating pain surged down her spine. Her body fell to the floor with convulsions caused by the chip embedded in her neck that rivaled any electrical current known to man or beast. The bones that had been as strong as steel for decades began to crack and break. First, every spinal vertebra, then her ribs and sternum, before finally her skull, arms, and legs. As the pain made its final descent through the tips of her fingers and toes, her eyes met Becca's. Even though she could see the pain and torment echoing in her daughter's eyes, she knew she had done the right thing.

The last sound she heard was the horrendous screams of the one she gave it all up for.

♌ ♈ ♉

Becca could barely breathe as her sobs racked her body. Lily was finally still, but Liam was moaning and slowly rolling around on his back.

Becca tried to calm herself as she watched Liam change. The large chunk of flesh that Lily tore from his neck was almost completely healed. His skin had taken on a pale luster while his hair seemed softer and developed more shine.

She counted his breaths, waiting and watching for the last one. He let out a low, almost guttural moan, as his last breath left his body. She only had a moment to take it all in before he began to move again.

Liam rolled from his back to his side and stretched his whole body. He twisted his ankles in a circular motion before setting his feet on the ground and jumping up into a crouch. He slowly got his bearings after the quick movement and stood straight up.

"Not exactly what I expected." Liam held his arms out in front of himself. He rolled up his sleeves, noticing the new definition to his forearms and slipped the sides of his shirt apart to take in his newly sculpted torso. His fingertips gently strummed the rigid planes of his abdomen as he closed his eyes in pure awe of his new self.

When he opened them, he turned to see Lily's crumpled and broken body as it lay next to Becca's feet.

"I am sorry for your loss, but it was necessary."

Becca squirmed as their eyes met.

"Don't worry, I'll-" Liam was cut off by a loud crash, seemingly just outside the room. "They're almost here. I can hear them breathing." He concentrated on listening to their incoming visitors. "That is my cue to leave, but it won't be for long. I have no doubt we will be seeing each other again." Liam laid a kiss on Becca's forehead as she struggled away.

Liam walked over to the side wall with a smile. "I've always wanted to do this." Liam punched through the concrete wall with ease. He kicked away enough of the wall to slip through before jumping out the hole and disappearing into the fading daylight.

Not even a second later, Abe busted through the door with Sam and Ryan. Abe was immediately at her side releasing her mouth from the gag.

"We have to help her." Her voice cracked as it struggled to regain its former tone.

"They'll take care of her, baby. Are you alright?" Abe was frantic as he removed her restraints and pulled her into his arms.

"No," she sobbed.

Abe rocked Becca back and forth in his arms as Ryan and Sam took in Lily's appearance.

"How long has she been like this?" Sam implored Becca.

"Not long." Becca gasped for breath as she tried to contain her sobs. "Maybe ten minutes?"

"There's still a chance. We need to get her back to the house." Sam helped Ryan lift Lily's body.

"Can I carry you, baby? We need to get out of here fast." Abe settled his hands on the side of Becca's face after sweeping her tear soaked tresses from her face.

"What about Ian?" She hiccuped then held her breath.

"We've searched the entire place. He's not here. We will send a team back to do a sweep, but we need to get you out of here now."

Becca nodded and Abe swept her up in his arms.

They all rushed out of the building to a safe distance then transported themselves back to Leatherby Manor.

They were greeted by Jefferson and Renee as they rushed into the front parlor. Ryan laid Lily on the couch and knelt down next to her.

"What's next? How do we fix her?" Ryan pleaded with Sam for answers.

"We need Peter." Abe stood stock still. His arms rigid at his sides, his head tilted slightly back, eyes clenched shut in concentration. A slight blue glow surrounded him as his concentration increased.

"You rang." Peter appeared out of nowhere standing beside the couch.

"Fix her!" Ryan screamed.

Peter took one look at Lily's broken body and knew what had happened.

"I knew that chip would bite us in the ass one day, but there is a way to reverse it. Blood."

Ryan began to pull up his sleeve to slash his wrist.

"No." Peter grabbed his forearm. "An angel's blood is too potent and a human's blood isn't enough."

"A Nephilim." Sam whispered.

"Yes. They might just have the right balance to bring her back. All of the injuries are internal, so the blood should be able to heal her from the inside out."

"But where...?" A cry tore from Ryan's chest as he sat on the couch, pulling Lily into his arms.

Peter turned his gaze to Becca where she was held tightly in Abe's arms.

"Me?" Becca questioned. "But I'm not-"

Peter cut her off, looking directly into her eyes. "Your father is an angel, Rebecca."

"Is?"

Peter turned his gaze to Sam. Shock and disbelief contorted his brow. "But Anne said I wasn't..."

Peter let out a soft laugh. "She lied."

Sam shook his head in disbelief before turning his eyes to meet Becca's. The instant they connected, he knew it to be true.

"Rebecca," Sam whispered. "I didn't know."

Becca let a soft smile cross her lips before she took a deep breath. She removed herself from Abe's embrace then laid a soft, chaste kiss on his lips. She turned to Peter with a sudden look of determination. "What do I need to do?"

Peter motioned for her to sit on the couch. He moved Lily's head to rest in Becca's lap while Ryan sat at Lily's feet.

"Her venom can't be transferred while she's in this state. Just let the blood flow down her throat." Peter took Becca's wrist and made an incision with his finger. He pressed the wound to Lily's mouth and let the blood flow down her throat.

After a few moments, Becca's head fell to the back of the couch from the blood loss.

Abe rushed to Becca's side. He laid soft kisses on her forehead and eyelids as he sat on the arm of the couch. "How much longer?" Abe turned to Peter.

Peter looked down to Lily's body. There were no breaths being taken like a human would, but the essence of life was slowly returning to her body. Her back slightly arched as her fingers trembled.

"It's working. I can feel her muscles moving." Ryan smiled as he brought Lily's hand to his lips.

Becca's head fell to the side as her body went limp.

"We need to stop." Sam knelt down before Becca. "She's fading too fast."

Peter took one last look over Lily and made the decision. He took Becca's wrist from Lily's mouth and sealed her wound.

"Get Becca to the nearest hospital. She is going to need a massive transfusion, soon." Peter waved his left hand above his right palm and a stack of papers appeared. "Just present these at Emergency and they will get her in immediately."

Sam took the papers as Abe gathered Becca in his arms before they both disappeared with her only a second later.

"Take Lily to bed. She will come around, but it might take hours. Maybe days." Ryan nodded before giving Lily a kiss and bringing her into his arms.

"What about Ian?"

"I'm heading off with a team from Manchester now. We'll find him."

Ryan nodded and was off up the stairs with his wife.

Jefferson held Renee as they stood back in shock at what had just transpired.

"Jefferson, I'm so sorry we had to meet again under these circumstances. Renee..."

"I guess you're not really her brother then, huh?" Renee asked.

Peter let out a soft chuckle as he shook his head back and forth. "No, but I wish I were at times." He went over to Jefferson and rested his hand on his shoulder. "Take care of things for me and I'll be in touch."

Jefferson nodded in acknowledgement as he held Renee tighter. Barely a second later, Peter was gone.

# Chapter Twenty One

## Accomplice

After what seemed like hours, Ian was on the brink of desperation. He had no idea when or even *if* Becca would be back. Liam made his innuendos, but Ian knew he could not trust him with his life. That brought him back to that fucking door.

He sat on the floor with his back resting up against the foot of the bed staring at the door, more importantly, the lock.

Becca had not explained what the Tersuline lock did, only that her last encounter with one had been disastrous. Even though he had been inundated with information about angels, demons, vampires, and all kinds of other worldly beings over recent days, he had no idea what to do with a magical lock that had managed to scare even Becca into staying put.

He looked around the room to see if there was anything that would remotely be of any use. Some food, empty water bottles, bed linens, and pillows were about it. He picked up a plastic water bottle and approached the lock just above the door handle.

He touched the bottle to the lock. Nothing. No melting or instantly bursting into flames like he had imagined might happen. Still, he didn't trust the powers at work to touch it with his bare hands. He went to the bed and removed a pillow from its case. He slipped his arm in and wrapped it around his arm up to his elbow. With trepidation, he reached for the handle. It was cool through the thin material of the pillowcase. He ventured forth to grip the handle and attempt a turn and was more than a little surprised when the handle gave and turned as he twisted it. He could feel the vibrations in the handle turning the gears of the lock as they slowly allowed the door to open. The handle was fully turned. He could feel himself pull the door open when he was overtaken by the incredible urge to scratch his forearm.

He placed his foot at the base of the door to keep it propped open and went to remove the pillowcase from his arm. His stomach wretched as thousands of green colored boils began popping up all over his forearm. He rushed to the bucket beside the bed and emptied what little he had in his stomach.

As soon as he had come to what he thought might be a conclusion, he noticed the boils breaking open and an opaque puss oozing from each one. The puss began dripping on to other parts of his body and soon enough his entire body was covered in boils. He writhed in agony for what felt like eternity until the puss dried and crusted up all over his body, making him feel as if he was covered in used sandpaper.

Once his body returned to a state of a dull ache as opposed to searing pain, he attempted to clear his thoughts. He wondered if the boils and puss were the disastrous consequences that Becca had spoken of. He wished to God he had have asked instead of letting it all lie.

Thoughts of Becca brought a tear to his eye. It dripped from the corner of his eye to quickly be absorbed by his new skin. He attempted to move, but his skin held him in place.

He spent hours just letting his thoughts wander to what his life with Becca could become to distract him from his discomfort. He wanted so much for every single thought to become a reality. A small, elegant wedding in the church he was christened in as a child, a romantic honeymoon to somewhere warm and secluded, followed by months of nights filled with trips for ice cream while their child grew within her. He saw himself sitting at the piano with a chubby-fingered little girl teaching her scales. Family picnics, baseball games, swim tournaments, second, third, and even possibly fourth honeymoons... All leading up to a day where they would watch their grandchildren run in the front yard while the neighborhood kids set off fireworks; him holding his loving wife in his arms while thinking of setting off some fireworks of their own.

It all came to a stop as the sound of the lock turned and the door opened. Ian braved the pain and turned his head to see a pair of very expensive hiking boots. His eyes slowly traveled upward to find the man standing in them.

Very tall from Ian's perspective, but that wasn't saying much. He could see the sharp jaw line and the shaggy blond hair, but could just barely make out the vibrant blue-gray eyes staring down at him.

"Mr. Holt. I've been waiting so long to meet you."

He circled around Ian's head and went to grab him underneath his arms. Ian cried out in pain as the man flung him onto the bed.

"It's too bad you had a little run in with my lock. I hope you will be strong enough to make the trip by this evening."

"Where are you taking me?" Ian felt the skin at the corners of his mouth tear and tasted the blood as it ran into his mouth.

"So excited, I see." The man sat down on the bed next to Ian. "I'll be taking you back to my birthplace."

Ian gently closed his eyes as he sat in confusion. He had no idea who this man was, but he was positive beyond any doubt that he was Liam's partner. Ian ventured to question what had happened to Liam.

"And Liam?"

"Liam has served his purpose for now. He got what he needed from Lily and is on his merry way to the path of death and destruction."

Ian felt like rolling his eyes at the way the man was talking in such riddles and half-truths.

"Becca?"

The man's eyes lit up like Christmas morning at the mention of her name, and a wave of nausea and guilt swept throughout his entire being.

"My Rebecca will be with us soon. That is what you want?" He lifted his brow as he looked down on Ian.

"Yes." Ian gulped at the possible implications of his answer.

"I know you love her – It's hard not to. I've loved that woman for so many years. The last time I had her, I made so many mistakes. Not this time. You, my dear boy, will change all that." A crooked smile crossed the man's lips before his tongue darted out to wet them.

Ian could hardly handle all of the emotions flowing through his body. He had no idea who this man was or what part he would play in the man's game. He waited for the man to just hurry up and explain already, but he just sat there in a slight daze. Ian closed his eyes tight, and then asked the question that had to be answered.

"Who are you?"

The man smiled down on him once again before running his hand through the hair on Ian's brow.

"Gideon."

His heart raced as the name floated from the man's lips. The body-stealing, murderer and rapist demon, who had an obsession with Becca, was the one hovering over him and getting ready to make Ian an intrinsic part of his plan to get Becca.

"Why haven't you just taken me over? It would have been a lot easier."

"Yes, it would have," Gideon sighed, before lying down on the bed beside Ian. "There is this little snag about being a demon in human form. My body only lasts about three hundred years, then I have to find a new one to take over my permanent being. I'm sitting at two hundred and ninety-nine and have lost my ability of possession. I thought I would possibly use Abe, but with his abilities and not being of natural human birth, it was not possible. But now that you have come into the picture just in time, I can transfer myself into your body – permanently."

Ian's fear took hold of his entire being as he started to shake uncontrollably.

"No, no, don't worry. It doesn't hurt. I just take you to my home, we make the transformation, and then you lay this body to rest. Simple." Gideon words were soft in what Ian thought was an awkward attempt at soothing his fears.

"What happens to me, to *my* mind and soul?"

Gideon took a deep breath before resting his head back to look towards the ceiling. "I will inherit most of your memories and will most likely take over your life, at least for a while. You will be in there somewhere – I might even be able to hear you on occasion – but you will have no control or say in what I do."

Gideon sat up from the bed and turned to Ian. "Anyway, we should get going. You should be healed by the time we could make it to the base."

"Base of what?"

"Hekla."

*Hekla? Hekla...* The name reverberated over and over in his mind as he searched for where he had heard it before. His mind brought him back to a conversation he once had with Lily about all her travels. Iceland had been one she mentioned a time or two. He had asked her why she would want to visit somewhere so cold with so many volcanoes. That is when she explained about Hekla and the belief that it was the gateway to Hell. He thought it silly at the time and had asked her why she believed in such a thing. She replied only that someone had to.

"The gateway to Hell?"

"Exactly."

"Shit." Ian squeezed his eyes shut with the realization that his life really was going straight to Hell.

# Chapter Twenty Two

## Silver And Gold

*T*he door creaked slightly as Renee entered the master bedroom suite. The noise caught Ryan's attention as he sat on the bed next to a stunningly still Lily.

"Anything?" Renee inquired, inching forward before making herself comfortable at the end of the bed.

"A few tremors here and there, but she hasn't opened her eyes yet." Ryan ran his hands over his face, his palms digging into his eye sockets. "I've been reading to her. It used to be her favorite." Ryan reached for the green, leather bound book. "During the day time, we would banter with other's words. The rest of the family thought we were immersing ourselves in the literature of the day, but it was really the only way we could speak without really speaking."

"Can you tell me what she was like? I can't really imagine her as a teenager." Renee was a bit giddy to find out a little more of the friend she realized she really knew nothing about.

Ryan shook his head and closed his eyes imagining the first time he saw Lily.

"When I was just thirteen, my father announced we would spend a year in Boston. I was horrible the entire journey. Back then we went by boat and it wasn't a short trip. I thought my father would murder me at several points as we sailed; but the moment I stepped off that boat and my eyes met hers, my whole life changed." Ryan began to get a little choked up as he remembered the ivory ribbons that had been woven into her hair that day. "It was an instant connection for both of us and we were inseparable as our fathers worked together for that entire year. My sisters adored her. My youngest sister, Beatrice, thought Lily hung the moon and that she was solely responsible for making the stars shine every night." Ryan's fingertips sought out his wife's cheek. He stroked them back and forth as the memories continued to flow. "She was interested in everything. Literature, science, history, and especially arithmetic... She was amazing with numbers. She loved how every problem had a finite solution; that numbers were the only thing in life where the answers never changed. I found it so fascinating that a girl so young could know so much. I learned more from her in that year than I ever had at home."

"But you went back?" Renee asked, as her eyes glistened with unspent tears.

"Yes. My heart felt like ash, destroyed and floating listlessly in the wind. We spent the next five years writing letters and promising we would meet again someday. The day my father sat me down and told me his dear friends had passed away, I begged him to let me go to her. Instead, he told me she would be coming to London to live with us – indefinitely. I was happier in that moment than I had ever been in my life, until I realized she was only coming because her parents had passed on." Ryan took Lily's hand in his and brushed his thumb across her knuckles.

"The day she arrived, I thought I must have died because she was my heaven. She had become a beautiful woman and I had grown out of my awkward adolescence. We made our pleasant hellos before she left to get settled. That night I found her in the stables. She told me how hard it was to sell her horse before coming to live with us. How hard it was giving up everything she had ever known to move across the ocean. I took her to mean she regretted her decision and was about to suggest I go back to Boston with her, when she surprised me with a confession of her own. She told me leaving was the best thing she could have ever done. If she couldn't be with her parents, the only other person in the world she wanted to be with was me." The corners of Ryan's mouth lifted slightly. "That was the perfect moment and I couldn't waste another second without having her in my arms. I pulled her to me and kissed her exactly how I had imagined I would since the second I saw her."

"How romantic," Renee sighed.

"It wasn't all flowers and rainbows, though. We were sure my parents would never approve of our relationship, and it took us seven years of sneaking around before we finally told them. My mother arranged the wedding so fast, both of our heads were spinning."

"It happened soon after that?"

"On our honeymoon. She fell from the train we were traveling on. I only just learned that a vampire found her and turned her straight away."

There was a knock at the door and Jefferson stepped in. "Sorry to interrupt, but Abe called. Becca has been in and out all night, but they think she's coming 'round."

"What about Peter?" Ryan asked.

Jefferson shook his head as he let out a soft laugh. "He's her doctor. Guess there's nothing that one can't do. I'll have to remember to stay on his good side."

"Yes, that's if you can handle what an incredible pain in the arse he is."

The mood in the room lightened a bit before Ryan looked down on Lily's face to see a soft smile gracing her lips. An air of hope coursed throughout the room as they all felt a new chapter of their lives was about to begin.

ଝ ᴡ ଷ

Abe had spent the hours at Becca's bedside doing what he had done over three years before – worrying she'd never be the same. The last time, she wasn't. She couldn't stand the sight of him. The man who had loved her for years, who had showed her the world, who would have given anything to be with her forever. The last time she woke from a hospital bed, his face terrified her and he was sure had haunted her nightmares for years.

Whenever she had stirred in her restless slumber, his touch seemed to calm her. He prayed with everything in him that this time would be different. That this time she would wake, see the love in his eyes, and make his world okay again.

Countless nurses and orderlies scurried in and out of the room throughout the day as bag after bag of blood was transfused. Abe stayed planted in his seat while Sam was in and out, checking and double checking whichever aspect of the investigation was going on.

"That should be the last one," the young female nurse with a bright smile and ginger hair stated matter of factually. "Her levels are all up. The doctor should be around shortly to discuss the plan with you."

"Thank you..." Abe looked to her name badge clipped on her scrub top. "Erin. I know Becca will appreciate how well she's being cared for when she comes around a little more."

"Not a problem. Just let me know if there is anything else you need. Otherwise, I'll be back to give her some medication in about an hour."

Abe nodded as Erin grinned before leaving the room.

He took Becca's hand and brought his forehead down to rest on her knuckles. He sat there praying and hoping a while longer before he felt her fingers twitch. He set her hand down and looked to see her droopy eyes staring back at him.

"Nice nap?"

Becca forced a weary smile. "As best I could on these mattresses. Even Liam gave us a decent bed, not that we ever got much sleep."

"Well." Abe shifted uncomfortably. "Sam is checking on everything. He thinks they found where you were being held."

"No Ian though?" Abe shook his head. "I don't have the energy to work this myself. You have to promise me you will do everything you can to help find him, especially after what I have to tell you."

Abe began to panic a bit. He wasn't sure he could handle the details of her relationship with Ian and was hoping against hope that she wouldn't subject him to that particular type of torture.

Becca lolled her head to the side to look Abe right in the eyes.

"You know Liam had a partner, right?"

"Yes, we figured he couldn't have known everything he had without someone guiding him."

"It was Gideon."

Abe suddenly stood, his chair falling to the floor behind him. "Holy fuck! I mean, shit..."

Becca laughed softly at Abe's unnatural swearing fit. Their entire time together, she could not remember a moment where he had even thought of uttering a curse word.

"Get it out." Abe looked down on her with a smile.

She continued to laugh a little louder until she tired from the movement.

"You never swear. It's nice to see you've loosened up a bit."

"Well..." Abe shrugged his shoulders before picking up the toppled chair and sitting back down. "Did Gideon possess Liam?"

"I don't think so, he just seemed to be giving the orders. Liam made sure to tell me that I would see him again before he busted through the wall. I'm afraid..." She gulped as she grabbed Abe's hand. "Gideon is back, and he's not going to give up this time."

Abe brought her fingers to his lips and kissed them with his eyes tightly squeezed shut. He took a deep breath, lowered her hand, and opened his eyes to look directly into hers.

"I failed you so horribly before, but I will not do it again. I will move heaven and earth to make sure you are safe. You know I can do it too." He smiled and gave her a wink.

"I know." She rolled her eyes before coming to a new realization. "Wait, what about me? Are there things I can do? You know, because of the half angel thing?"

"That would be a question for Sam or Peter. They've both been here on and off so I'm sure they can help with all your questions."

Becca relaxed into the stiff mattress while gazing into Abe's eyes. She knew that she could count on him to try. She was so tired of being angry with him and being angry with herself. Even with her burgeoning feelings for Ian, she knew her story with Abe wasn't over.

She gave his hand a squeeze just as her room door swung open and the face of a woman who was a great influence in both of their lives walked through.

"Imagine my surprise to get a call from my friends at Manchester telling me my best agent was indeed not on vacation, but had been kidnapped yet again by another psychopath."

The woman stood at the bedside tapping her toe against the linoleum floor waiting for answers. Her deep brown eyes and short, dark caramel hair framed her seemingly angered features just as Abe had remembered them.

"Director Palmire, we just-" Abe spoke, but was interrupted by the woman's raised hand.

"When did we get so formal? It's Marla. You remember that, don't you, Abe?"

Abe was pulled out of his chair and into the arms of the one and only Marla Palmire, Deputy Director of the FBI. She was one of the few members of the FBI that liaised with The Manchester Group, hence the close relationship with both Becca and Abe.

"Turns out its kind of the same psychopath," Becca spoke up, as her fingers twisted in her blanket.

"Gideon?" Marla sat down on the edge of the bed as the question hung in the air.

Becca looked to Abe with tear-filled eyes, then back to Marla with a small nod.

"Oh, honey." Marla gathered Becca into her arms as Becca attempted to control her sobs. "That bastard is not getting away with anything this time. Now that we have a Senator on our side, I don't think he has a chance."

"Senator Holt?" Becca pulled back to question.

"Yes. He's never been directly involved with Manchester, but since one of the largest firms is in his state, he's aware of its existence. He's actually the reason I'm here. He's outside."

Becca and Abe both lowered their heads and let out a soft string of swear words.

"No need to worry, everything you say is off the record. He's been briefed on how this works. Now, he just really wants to know what happened to Ian." Marla took Becca's hand while lifting her eyebrows, looking for some sort of approval.

"Sure." She looked over to Abe. "I think...maybe, I should do this on my own." Becca's heart ached in confusion. She had loved Abe for a great deal of her life, but then Ian appeared and for a split second, Abe was replaced. She knew Senator Holt would have questions she just wouldn't be able to answer in front of Abe.

"I'll be just outside. Marla and I need to catch up anyway." Abe leaned over and kissed her forehead before whispering, "I'll be here whenever you need me."

Silently, Abe led Marla out of the room. Becca heard a few muffled voices before a tall gentleman entered sheepishly.

"Rebecca?"

"Senator Holt, please sit."

"It's Bradford." He slipped his black overcoat off his shoulders before sitting in the chair Abe had recently vacated.

"Then you can call me Becca." She attempted a smile, but the exhaustion of the past hour was catching up to her.

"I won't keep you long. I still have a lot of information to absorb; I'm not sure how much more I can handle." He laughed softly and a pang struck directly at Becca's heart.

"You laugh just like him or, I guess, he laughs just like you," she sniffled, as she brought her hand to her chest in attempt to rub the ache out.

"Since the day he was born, everyone has said he's my miniature."

"I can see why." She tried to calm her nerves, but sitting only feet from an older version of Ian made her concentration less than stellar.

"I just need to know if you think he'll be alright."

Becca closed her eyes as she nodded, taking a deep breath before launching into her story. "I told Ian everything."

Becca told Bradford about their first phone call, their first dinner, and then the trip to Manchester. She explained how he willingly went with her and Sam to Iceland after he found out about Lily and her past, and told him how Liam had kept them away from Sam, knowing there was no way out.

"Let me make sure I've got this right." Bradford sat back and steepled his fingers in front of his chin. "You tell my son that your mother, the woman he's desperately in love with, is a vampire, then you both go off to Manchester, which is basically supernatural headquarters, looking for clues? Then, you leave for Iceland together, before being kidnapped and held hostage naked, when he realizes he loves you instead... Now the vampire is in a coma, you're down several pints, and your father's an angel, making you half angel. I got it all?"

"That about sums it up in a nutshell," she replied, smiling as much as she could in her weakened state.

"What's next?" Bradford questioned, as he raised an eyebrow to Becca. "We find Ian."

*Redemption*

# Chapter Twenty Three
## Welcome To Hekla

Ian spent most of the journey from England to Iceland in and out of consciousness. He fought to stay awake, but the pain from the healing of his skin often caused him to just pass out. The most he could make out was that he and Gideon had boarded a private jet at some point, and were currently making their way back to Iceland.

When he would rouse, he noticed Gideon smiling over at him from his seat across the aisle. He could occasionally make out a few words here and there, but the pain had been so intense that moving, speaking, or even thinking was out of the question at that point.

He was jostled awake fully when he felt Gideon lifting him up.

"Where are we?" Ian asked, his voice hoarse and throat incredibly sore.

"We're close. We have to go on foot from here on out."

Ian let his vision return to normal then surveyed his surroundings. He was standing beside a black SUV on snow covered ground. He turned to see that they were not far from the base of what he was sure was Hekla, the Queen of Iceland's volcanoes.

"Why here?" Ian turned to see Gideon admiring the volcano. "Is there some reason it has to be here?"

Gideon took a deep breath, filling his aging lungs with the scent of the volcanic ash. "Since my beginning, this is always the place where I have come to rest. This body will join my others, as will yours someday. This is where my father brought me to life and it is where my power was born. The humans have their theories and superstitions, but most are far from the truth."

"So, this isn't the gateway to Hell?" Ian approached Gideon with a slight groan as his skin still stung with the slightest movement.

"Oh no, well... Actually, they were right about that one. It's not something you could just stumble over, mind you. You need special skills that no human could ever posses to gain entrance." Gideon placed his hand on Ian shoulder and gave it a slight squeeze. "It's time."

That was the lowest moment of Ian's life. It was the moment he gave up – as he was no match for Gideon's powers. He knew no one was coming to rescue him, and he knew, without a shadow of a doubt, he would soon be standing on Hell's doorstep.

The pain that began to radiate throughout his body was no longer from the healing of his skin. His entire body was wracked with only what he could attempt to name as heartache. His whole being mourned at the loss of his future; of never seeing his family again, never kissing the woman he loved, never holding his child or grandchild... It was the most atrocious feeling one could have, to lose all hope, to know that your forever was about to end.

His feet led him without his brain telling them to do so. He made it up the steep rock face, across jagged volcanic rock ledges, and up to the cavern where Gideon had finally stopped.

"Not too much further." Gideon walked in front of him towards a light glowing in red and amber hues.

Ian's stoic movements continued as the light got closer and brighter, before the light went out and both were cast into darkness.

"Gideon, son of our Father, demanding entrance!" Gideon shouted as loud as he could. His voice echoed off the cavern walls for several moments before the light returned.

"See," Gideon said as he smacked Ian on the chest. "They know me here."

The two of them entered through the lit doorway into a separate smoldering hot cavern.

"It's best to just take off your clothes. The heat can be unbearable to humans at times, but we'll change that soon enough."

Ian began to disrobe without thought while Gideon just removed his shirt.

Gideon came to stand before a completely bare Ian.

"It won't hurt much. Just a few moments and it will all be over."

Gideon held Ian's inner arm and took a palm-sized volcanic rock to slice into his flesh from elbow to wrist. Gideon handed the rock to Ian and instructed him to do the same on Gideon's inner arm. Ian did so without a second of hesitation.

The rock was placed off to the side and Gideon placed their inner arms together; blood to blood, flesh to flesh. Warmth traveled throughout both of them as the blood flowing between them began to boil. Pain from the heat brought both of them to their knees, but their connection could not be broken. Ian felt as though Gideon's arm was melding with his own. When he regained enough of his faculties to open his eyes, he could see that was exactly what was happening. Gideon's arm and hand were being absorbed by Ian's as their blood brought them together.

Gideon's body fell away as the arm and hand were completely absorbed.

Ian's eyes turned to see Gideon's lifeless body. He attempted to rise from his knees to his feet, but instead he found himself crawling on all fours towards the body. Ian protested, attempting to force his brain to send the signal to make him stand, but it was as if he was shouting into an abyss where no sound was heard.

Ian blinked several times and felt tears falling from his own eyes. His lips kissed each of Gideon's closed eyelids.

"You were a good vessel, my brother. Now you will lay in peace as your reward."

Ian could hear the voice leaving his body as his own, but had no control over its actions. It had worked. Gideon had completely taken over his mind and body, yet he could still see, hear, and feel everything around him. There was no way that could be right.

Gideon, now controlling Ian's every move, picked up his old body and moved it closer to the glowing light which turned out to be a slow flowing river of lava. He tossed the body in and watched as it was consumed by the molten river. He sighed one last time before gathering all the clothes and redressing his new body.

Ian continued to shout as his body made its way back down the volcano's face and soon, the SUV was back in sight. One journey had come to an end and another had just begun.

ଝ ⅋ ୫

Ian really had no idea how to feel. He was trapped in a dark corner of his mind that wasn't even his own anymore. He could scream and yell, but it did no good. Either Gideon couldn't hear him or chose not to.

He wondered if that was how he was going to spend the next three hundred years, seeing, hearing and feeling the world but not ever experiencing it for himself. It had only been a few hours and he could already feel himself being driven mad.

Gideon finally brought the SUV to a stop as he reached the small landing strip where the plane was waiting for him. He began humming softly as he exited the SUV then walked with a slight swagger over to the steps to board the plane.

"We are ready for takeoff. Just take your seat and relax. We will be landing outside London on schedule, Mr. Holt."

"Thank you." Gideon nodded to the pilot with a smile before he took his seat.

Ian's mind raced as he realized they were returning to England. Gideon was going after Becca. He was going to take over Ian's life.

Gideon began humming the tune again as the plane took to the air. Ian began to concentrate on the sound and realized that it was his own composition – one that had never left his mind. Ian thought about the rage he would go into if he could. The complete violation and destruction of his entire world was more than he could fathom. He curled up into a ball in that dark corner that was no longer his own mind and attempted to forget.

ଛ ᛦ ଅ

Ian came out of his darkness when he began to feel incredibly strange. Gideon was standing face to face with the pilot, when all of a sudden, he fell to the floor of the plane's cabin.

Ian thought Gideon had received some sort of shock as the energy surged through their body. Eyelids blinked rapidly over tear-filled eyes as everything came back into focus.

Fingertips massaged at temples as the pain still surged, footsteps were heard descending the stairs of the plane. Everything was so muddled, but getting back into the seat was not too difficult.

"What the hell was that?" Ian asked to the empty cabin.

Hearing his own voice matching his own thoughts caught him completely off guard. Ian told himself to stand, he stood. He told himself to sit, he sat. All actions were done rather sluggishly, but they were under his own control all the same.

He reasoned that Gideon must have left his body to possess the pilot. What he hadn't expected was that he would be able to have back control of his body when Gideon left it. Weak, but in control, hope returned as he began to believe his forever hadn't ended after all.

# Chapter Twenty Four

## Property

After Senator Holt had left, Becca was alone and actually conscious. It had been a long while since that had been the case. Her mind was scattered in so many different directions, to put them all in order would be a daunting task.

Her first thought was of Lily. She knew why Lily had given herself up. Lily walked into that room with Liam knowing full well that she would not be able to deny his request. Even if the connection that Liam and Lily shared wasn't there, Becca was sure Lily would have gone through with it anyway. But Becca prayed in that moment, to the Big Guy, to Peter and to her mother, that everything they had gone through was not in vain. Lily had to be alright, she still had so much more to do.

Next were her thoughts of Ian and their last moments together. Her chest ached as she remembered his touch, his kiss, and the feel of his skin against hers. She not only felt a connection with Ian, but with his father as well. Ian was truly his father's son – they were a matched pair. Speaking with Bradford and listening to his stories of his son had put her a little at ease, but not enough to reveal her last moments with his son to him.

Then there was Abe – strong, valiant, and always handsome Abe. When she looked at him now, there was no fear. She only saw the love he had given her for some of the best years of his life emanating from his entire being. That feeling on its own made her world so much more confusing. She knew he loved her and she had to admit to herself, that deep down, she still loved him too.

A tear slipped down her cheek as she stood staring out her hospital window, and was slightly startled when a large, warm thumb wiped it from her cheek. She turned to stare into the sparkling blue eyes of her father.

"Dad." She turned into him and wrapped herself up in his embrace.

He sighed after he kissed the top of her head. "I'm here. I'm finally here."

"I know." She squeezed him tighter as she let several more tears fall.

"I always suspected, but Anne told me I wasn't and I accepted her word. I'm sorry I never pressed it. Your life could have been so different if you had been with me."

"Hey." She stepped back from his embrace. "My life hasn't been roses and cotton candy, but I have a lot to be proud of. Despite everything that happened with Gideon and my relationship with Abe, I'm a damn good agent, a wonderful friend, and I hope to add doting daughter to that list."

"I hope so too." Sam kissed her forehead before bringing her over to sit on the bed with him. "I'm sure you have some questions."

"Several." She rolled her eyes as she blew out a tuft of air.

"I'll answer what I can, so go for it." Sam held onto her hand as he waited for the inquisition to begin.

"I guess the big one is, what am I? I mean, what can I do?" She looked up to him with more than just those questions in her eyes.

"Well, I told you that a child of an angel and a human is called a Nephilim. As far as what angelic attributes you might possess, one has always been very evident."

"What is that?" she questioned, truly intrigued.

"Your ethereal beauty."

Becca ducked her head and couldn't help the blush that rose to her cheeks. "I'm nothing compared to Lily."

"That is not true. You have always been so beautiful. You have your mother's hair coloring, and now I know for sure where you got those amazing blue eyes."

She let out a soft laugh. Her eyes were the one thing she was always complimented on. "I love my eyes. So, thank you for that."

"No problem." He chuckled. "But the other traits you can inherit from me are your choice."

"My choice?" This confused her. Wasn't an angel just an angel?

"Nephilim's have been on Earth for hundreds of thousands of years. Since the very first was born, God has offered them free will. Things like the beauty and intelligence are inherited gifts, but talents such as teleportation and healing powers are only bestowed when you make the conscious decision to accept them."

"Some people don't?" Becca couldn't imagine why someone wouldn't want to.

"Well, they are only able to receive them once they consciously learn that one is indeed a Nephilim and are given the choice. Some don't find out who they are until much later in their lives and by then, they don't see a use for them. Some never find out at all." He shrugged his shoulders, not really sure how to explain the rationale of those that choose a different path.

"What would be my gift, if I chose to receive one?" She arched her brow while biting nervously on her bottom lip.

"You would inherit my trait which is the power of healing."

"Healing? Would I be able to heal myself or just others?"

"It only works on humans, but if it makes you feel better, once you receive your gift you become somewhat invincible." He smiled while imaging his daughter as some sort of superhero.

"Even from Gideon?" She knew the answer, but she asked anyway.

"No, but we are working on keeping you as far away as possible."

"What about Ian? I promised his father we would find him."

Sam stood then turned back to face her. "If you're ready, we can take that first step today."

"You've found something?" she asked, as she stood before him.

"We found where you were held. We have some questions. Once we get you released, would you be willing to come check it out with me?"

She began to search the room for anything suitable to wear into the outside world. "How fast can Peter get me out of here?"

Sam crossed his arms and laughed as her search became frantic. "That's my girl."

"Getting reacquainted, I see." Abe grinned as he entered the room, closing the door softly behind him.

"Get Peter to get me out of here. And where on God's green earth are my clothes?" Becca slammed the empty closet door as she turned back to Abe and Sam.

Abe pulled the shopping bag from behind his back and offered it up as it dangled from his index finger. "I hope it's all to your liking."

Becca took a deep, calming breath before reaching for the bag. "Thank you." She took a look in the bag to find shoes, jeans, a few shirts, and matching bra and underwear. "You picked these out?" She raised an eyebrow to Abe with a slight smile.

Abe chuckled, as he was sure she was remembering his fascination with her undergarments. When they were together, she had dressers full of items he had purchased for her and were for his eyes only.

"I hope they are all right."

"You always did know what I like," she replied, as she began to pull each item out of the bag. She stopped and looked to the two men observing her. "If you hadn't noticed, I'm going to change. So why don't you two go get things settled with Peter so I can get out of here."

"Yes, ma'am." Abe shook his head back and forth with a smile as he opened the door.

Sam kissed Becca on the cheek before exiting with Abe.

The two men found Peter chatting up the nurses not far from Becca's room.

"Excuse us, doctor. May we have a word about Miss Swift?" Sam said in his most professional voice.

"Yes, of course. Excuse me ladies." Peter led Sam and Abe over to one of the waiting rooms.

"She's changing now. I'm taking her to see the space we think she was held in." Sam stated.

Peter waved his hand over his palm and produced a set of discharge paperwork. "Here. Make sure she drinks plenty of fluids and gets enough rest."

"Yes, doctor." Abe snickered.

"Just let me know when she has made her decision. I'll be waiting."

"Of course." Sam nodded as Peter took a few steps away from them and disappeared into thin air.

"Decision?" Abe questioned.

"Her powers. I explained to her that she would inherit the same abilities that I possess."

"Did you discuss the limitations?"

Sam shook his head. "We hadn't made it to that part yet. I'll explain after we go and check this place out."

Becca peeked around the corner into the waiting room to find Abe and Sam. "Have you sprung me yet?"

Sam lifted the pile of paperwork still in his hand. "All set."

"Then let's get this over with, I want to get back to Lily. Any word?"

Sam sighed. "I talked with Jefferson a while ago. Still just a few tremors here and there."

"All the more reason we get this over with. Are you coming with us?" Becca turned to ask Abe.

"Definitely."

ও ᛉ ঙ

Becca stepped into the room where she had last seen Ian. It was on the top floor of a house that was only five kilometers away from Leatherby Manor. From the outside, no one would ever guess the horrors that lay within.

An agent was snapping pictures of small scenes with little numbered tags beside each one. Another was dusting different surfaces for fingerprints. She laughed a bit to herself knowing none of it would do any good.

She took long, deep breaths as she took in the room before turning back to the door. It was at that moment she discovered the Tersuline lock was missing from the door; that a lock, period, was missing. A large hole now resided where the deadly device had once been.

"Where is it?" Becca asked, as she walked to the door and ran her fingers over the edges of the hole.

"Tersuline?" Sam questioned and she nodded as she continued examining the hole. "It appears it was blown off. A small explosion would do the trick, I think."

"Did they find any blood?" She turned back to address everyone in the room.

"No blood, just this." Sam pointed to a spot on the floor covered with a puss like substance. "We will do some DNA testing, but were certain it came from Ian."

Visions of Rome came to the forefront of her mind. Her writhing on the floor in agony for hours while she waited for someone to save her. The memory of her skin literally falling from her body in chunks caused gooseflesh to sweep across every inch of her body.

"I should have explained what would happen. I didn't get the chance and who knows what condition he's in now."

Abe pulled her into his arms, and she accepted his comfort even though it felt so wrong. In that moment, she knew her world would never be the same. She was in love with two men – two men who had the ability to turn her world into her own private hell. She'd been there before and she had the distinct feeling she was crawling back with every breath she took.

# Chapter Twenty Five

## Unknown

"Who are you?" Becca asked the man who sat in vigil at Lily's bedside.

"With everything going on, it seems we neglected to explain." He looked to Peter who was loitering in the doorway. "I'm Lily's husband, Ryan."

Shock confronted her features as she took in his. She should have realized on sight who he was. He was exactly how Lily had always described. The hair, the jaw line, the eyes...all perfect replicas of the image she created had in her mind the first time Lily had shared their story.

"It's nice to finally meet you, but how?" She turned to look at Peter. "Did you have something to do with this?"

Peter smiled as he entered the room fully. "They've both worked for me in one way or another over the years, but it was just recently I learned of their, um...connection."

"Of course." Becca nodded her head as she made it to the opposite side of the bed from Ryan. She lay down on the bed and curled herself into Lily's side like she had done so many times in her life.

She closed her eyes as she began to reach for Lily's hand. With their fingers intertwined, Becca began to recount her days since she set foot in Boston.

Ryan and Peter listened from the corner of the room as Becca retold every detail, including her burgeoning feelings for Ian and the return of the spark she had once felt with Abe. She whispered with a few tears as she admitted how incredibly terrified she was of what Gideon had in store for her next.

She pleaded with Lily to wake, only to receive a small squeeze of her hand. But it was enough for now. She knew Lily was in there somewhere and had heard every word.

After several hours of hearing her own voice, Becca was lulled into a peaceful sleep at Lily's side.

ଧ ⅋ ଌ

He rushed to his office and pulled up the video feed from Leatherby Manor as soon as he got the signal that Lily's chip had been activated. He watched as she was brought in and placed delicately on the living room sofa. He watched as her Becca's blood was freely given as a sacrifice, an attempt to bring back into being someone who by all forces of nature, should not exist in the first place. He clawed at his face as he read the pain in all of their eyes as they went back and forth through her room. When Becca entered the room and curled into Lily's side, anger, frustration, and physical pain surged through every cell of his undead body. As each moment passed with little to no sign of life, he felt his un-beating heart being torn in two.

He'd had enough. He ripped his black suit jacket from the back of his chair and marched out of his office, past his secretary and the hundreds of subordinates who had no clue who he really was or his current mission.

"He's not available," the young woman cried, as he stomped past her and into the largest office in the building.

"He's available to me!" he screamed, before he slammed the door behind him, shattering it into a million pieces.

"I see you're up to date with the situation in Reading," the elderly man stated from behind his solid mahogany desk.

"It's been days. Please, just let me do it." He hated to beg, but Mr. Manchester was the only man who had the power to do what needed to be done.

"We did this for your own good. Your race was a mistake for so many reasons. The four of you aside, eradicating your race was the best thing to ever happen. Could you imagine what would have become of this world if we had let you all continue to roam free?"

"No, Mr. Manchester. I can't." The man took one more gulp of air before launching into another plea. "She's the only one who will be able to deal with Liam. She knows him on a cellular level now. She can find him and deal with him before it gets out of hand."

"There is another and you damn well know it," Mr. Manchester retorted with a huff.

"Archer?" The man laughed. "Nathaniel Archer has zero real world experience. He wouldn't know his ass from his elbow if he didn't have an instruction card in his pocket." The man shook his head softly from side to side at the outrageous notion Mr. Manchester was presenting.

Mr. Manchester rubbed his hands over his porcelain smooth face in frustration. From that day so many decades ago when their plan was enacted, Mr. Manchester knew he might have to make this very decision. They had put a backup plan in place that only he and the man standing in front of him knew about.

"I've changed the codes again. Come with me and we can get started."

Mr. Manchester maneuvered from behind his desk and motioned for the man to follow.

They walked at a steady pace through the halls and tunnels of the London office of The Manchester Group, before Mr. Manchester slowed as they made it to the laboratory level to enter his codes into the identification panel. Both he and his companion supplied blood samples before completing a retinal scan. The extensive verification process completed, they entered the lab and began gathering the equipment together to begin "Project Rejuvenation".

"Can you pull up the video feed on your mobile?" Mr. Manchester asked, as he began uncovering the large computer console.

"Of course." The man pulled out his cell phone, pushing several buttons and waiting a few moments for things to load before the screen showed Lily lying with a sleeping Becca at her side.

The whirr of the console startled the man as Mr. Manchester brought it back to life. With almost ten minutes of key strokes and several wipes of his sweat soaked brow, Mr. Manchester was finally able to begin.

"We need to do it together," Mr. Manchester instructed. "On my mark." Both men made ready at the two switches before them. "Three...Two...One..." The switches flipped and each man held his breath watching the small screen.

ଛ ᛦ ଛ

Ryan, Sam, and Abe entered the master bedroom not at all surprised to see Becca still curled up at Lily's side.

"She took that same position every night for over a year following Anne's death." Sam sighed as he could see the pain etched in his daughter's face even in her slumber.

"They are quite a pair. Never one without the other," Abe commented, as he crossed his arms at his chest.

Ryan nodded with a smile. He imagined his own nights calming his nephew from one of his many nightmares. Sometimes being close to one another was the only thing that could be done to keep the demons at bay.

Becca stirred and sat up looking down at Lily with confusion warping her features.

"What is it?" Abe rushed to Becca's side.

"She shocked me then started shaking."

They watched as Lily slowly shook, and her entire body began to vibrate. With each second that passed the intensity increased. Within a moment, she was writhing off the bed.

Becca's eyes met Sam's with a plea for help, but even he had no clue what was occurring right before their eyes.

A blood curdling scream tore from Lily's throat, causing Becca to jump from the bed and into Abe's arms. The scream seemed to last for hours until finally Lily's voice and body came to rest.

Ryan knelt down at Lily's side, his hand gathered her own. He noticed her skin was a bit warmer, the sheen to it a bit softer. He looked to her eyes and saw her dark lashes slightly flutter before they slowly opened, showing him the most beautiful sight in the entire universe.

"Welcome back, my sweet," Ryan whispered, before placing a soft kiss on her more than perfect lips.

Lily gathered her strength and was able to whisper, "Becca?"

"I'm right here." Becca came back to the bed to lay behind her in a spooning position.

"I'm home." Lily's smile was reflected in Ryan's glistening eyes. "Finally home."

♌ ♍ ♎

The vodka flowed freely between the two men as they sat in their suite of the finest hotel in all of Bucharest. The television was all but background noise until the two men heard the language turn from Romanian to English.

"Turn it up." The man with chin length jet black hair and matching eyes said to the other.

The man with light caramel colored skin and chocolate brown, messy hair turned the volume up as he eyed his friend. The name Marla Palmire flashed across the screen as the woman stood with authority at the podium.

"This case has the full dedication of the American Embassies in the United Kingdom and Iceland, as well as the United States Federal Bureau of Investigations and the international law enforcement agencies in all three countries. The details of this case are being handled internally and we all hope the press would show respect for all parties involved." She turned and looked to her side before continuing. "Now, I will hand over to Senator Bradford Holt to give a brief statement on behalf of his family." Marla stepped to the side of the podium to make way for the imposing figure to her left.

A man in his mid fifties came on screen with a woman the two assumed was his wife by the way he was holding her. The press threw questions at them left and right.

"Our son, Ian, was last seen at the Reykjavik Airport on January third. The local authorities, along with the FBI are doing everything they can to pick up his trail, but have little to go on."

"He was traveling with another woman. What's happened to her?" A male reporter yelled at the man.

"She was recovered and is currently in a stable condition in London. All we have been able to obtain from her was that she was separated from Ian before she ended up in her current condition. I'm sorry, that is all I know about her."

"Please," the wife sobbed. "If anyone has any information that will lead to our son's return, there is a two million dollar reward."

The reporters continued to yell questions at the couple, but the men had heard enough. The television was shut off as they each quietly took a drink while absorbing the information.

The door to their suite opened and closed before a young, pale man stood before them.

"You need a little sun, Liam? You look white as a sheet." The two men laughed while Liam stood rolling his newly darkened eyes at them.

"It's done. Lily is dead. What is the next step?" Liam walked to stand before the two men.

"Debir, why don't you get the boy a drink and we will fill him in."

Debir stroked his fingers through his messy locks before reaching for a pint of crimson liquid. He poured it into a crystal goblet and handed it to Liam.

"It's the best way to drink if the source is unavailable." Debir smiled wickedly as he passed the goblet to Liam.

Liam took a long, languid drink. The blood saturated his tongue before rejuvenating each and every fiber of his being.

"It's been a little longer than we expected. Where have you been?"

"I wasn't able to get a hold of the Anarcori before I left, so I had to use human means of transportation. Between not slaughtering every human in my path and staying out of sight, it took longer than I expected." Liam sunk into a nearby chair and relaxed his head back.

"It's all well. We still have a while before we can begin. Right, Filipp?"

Filipp stood tall, his dark eyes piercing Liam's. "Absolutely, Debir. We have much to teach you, young Liam. Our years of searching for the perfect vessel to take down our enemy are at an end. Liam will join us now in his rightful place as an Ahbmonite elder. We will restore the vampire line and destroy every single entity the Manchester Group has ever touched."

Filipp lifted his shirt sleeve to gaze upon his birthright. His thumb circled the circular mark of black flames realizing that for the first time in decades, he would soon be rid of all things Manchester, including the small piece of metal and wires that was embedded at the base of his neck.

# Chapter Twenty Six

## Belfast, Ireland 1973

Lily lowered her camera to take in the view of the man who was her father, her mentor, and most importantly, her best friend.

"That one is going in the foyer. I'll find one of those printing shops that will make it the size of a poster that you would see outside of the cinema," she laughed, as she moved her thumb against the small wheel to wind the film.

"No one wants to see my ugly mug as soon as they walk in the door." Martin jumped off the rock he was standing on to lead Lily over to a nearby bench.

"I do." She smiled softly at him before looking back down at her camera.

"So, is photography your new obsession? No more chemistry and physics lessons?" Martin raised a thick, dark brow in her direction.

"I don't know. I like it. I know the powers that be and all the higher ups at Manchester want me to continue being the head of Research and Development here, but I'm getting an itch to move on. Aren't you?"

Martin took Lily's camera from her lap and set it down beside her. He slid his hand into hers before bringing it to his lips. "You know I'll follow you to the ends of the earth, my girl. I just have a feeling that we should stay put."

Lily's grasp tightened around his hand. "No, not yet."

Martin turned to her and cupped her cheek. "I'm sorry. I'm so sorry." He brought his lips down to her forehead to lay down a gentle kiss. "It's time to begin."

Lindsey Gray

*The persons places and things of Redemption*

*Persons*

**Abe North:** Agent for the Manchester Group, a fallen angel working his way up the ranks. Is known as a shadow walker – an angel who can transport beings to any spot in the universe with a single touch. Has the ability to see events that have occurred in a space like playing back a movie on a screen. Had a committed relationship with Becca Swift and is still very much in love with her.

**The Ahbmonites:** A race of humans whose blood has a special connection with vampires. They were used as feeders for vampires. With each feeding they gained vampiric traits. When they became too powerful, they were either turned or killed.

**Bradford and Marian Holt:** Ian's parents who have incredible influence in American politics and government.

**Debir and Filipp:** Two male vampires working for The Manchester Group. Used Liam to get rid of Lily so they could have the upper hand and begin their crusade to destroy The Manchester Group.

**Gideon:** A demon with the powers of possession and foresight. Has been obsessed with Rebecca Swift since she was a child.

**Ian Holt:** Twenty-nine year old son of the senator of Massachusetts, Bradford Holt and Marian Holt. Obtained his Masters degree in Piano Performance from The Boston Conservatory and is a professional concert pianist.

**Jefferson:** The human caretaker of Leatherby Manor. His family has worked for either Martin or Lily for decades.

**Liam Caldwell:** Last surviving member of the Ahbmonites. Stalked Lily from Las Vegas to Boston, then from Iceland to England, under the direction of Gideon and guidance of Debir and Filipp.

**Lily Edwards:** Only female vampire in known existence. Born December 31st, 1879. Married Ryan Edwards Spring 1905. Sired by Martin Leatherby in the Spring of 1905. She adopted the daughter of Anne Swift, Becca, when Becca was eight years old. Among her several degrees, she holds a Masters in Chemistry, and has been a member of The Manchester Group since the 1920's. Among other abilities, she is able to absorb heat.

**Lior:** Martin's sire. A born member of the Ahbmonite race.

**Marla Palmeri:** Deputy Director of the F.B.I. Becca's direct supervisor.

**Martin Leatherby:** Lily's sire and father figure.

**Mr. Manchester:** The president and founder of The Manchester Group.

**Nathaniel Archer:** To be revealed in "Revisited".

**Peter:** An Archangel. Messenger between the Big Guy and The Manchester Group.

**Rebecca "Becca" Swift:** Thirty-one year old adopted daughter of Lily. Special Agent with the FBI in Portland, Oregon. Had a committed relationship with Abe North.

**Renee:** Lily's best friend in Iceland. She owns the local tavern.

**Ryan Edwards:** An Angel of Death. Born October 2nd, 1879 and died Spring of 1927. Married Lily Edwards in Spring 1905. Adopted his sister's son, Denning, in 1916.

**Sam Fleming:** Head of The Manchester Group's Boston branch. A fallen angel working to repair his status in the heavenly ranks. Among his angel powers he also has the ability to heal human ailments.

*Places*

**Boston, Massachusetts:** Lily's birthplace and where she has kept a home for several decades. One of several locations that house a branch of The Manchester Group.

**Portland, Oregon:** Where Becca is stationed with the FBI.

**Reading, England:** Location of Leatherby Manor.

**Seltjarnarnes, Iceland:** The small town where Lily has a cabin that she escapes to every year. Home of Renee.

*Things*

**An Anarcori:** A red orb incased in a gold box which when activated, can transport a group of people from one place to another.

**Tersuline Lock:** A lock used to contain humans and other beings. If touched, causes boils to form all over the skin with eventual debilitating pain as the skin heals.

CPSIA information can be obtained at www.ICGtesting.com
Printed in the USA
BVOW080604110713

325560BV00003B/838/P